the stitch clique

Gracie Opens Shop

the stitch clique

Gracie Opens Shop

by tina wells

illustrations by mike segawa

WEST
MARGIN
PRESS

WEST MARGIN PRESS
AN IMPRINT OF TURNER PUBLISHING COMPANY
Nashville, Tennessee
www.turnerpublishing.com

WEST
MARGIN
PRESS

Gracie Opens Shop: The Stitch Clique

This is a work of fiction. All the characters and events portrayed in this book are either products of the author's imagination or are used fictitiously.

Book and cover design by William Ruoto
Illustrations by Mike Segawa

Library of Congress Cataloging-in-Publication Data
Names: Wells, Tina, author.
Title: Gracie opens shop / Tina Wells ; illustrations by Mike Segawa.
Description: Nashville, Tennessee : West Margin Books, [2023] | Series:
   Stitch clique ; 3
Identifiers: LCCN 2023005296 (print) | LCCN 2023005297 (ebook) | ISBN
   9781513139326 (hardcover) | ISBN 9781513141589 (paperback) | ISBN
   9781513141596 (epub)
Subjects: CYAC: Friendship--Fiction. | Business enterprises—Fiction. |
   Fashion—Fiction. | LCGFT: Novels.
Classification: LCC PZ7.W46846 Gr 2023 (print) | LCC PZ7.W46846 (ebook) |
   DDC [Fic]—dc23
LC record available at https://lccn.loc.gov/2023005296
LC ebook record available at https://lccn.loc.gov/2023005297

Printed in China

one

"Gracie Girl," Grace Alexander-Cline's mama groans from across the dinner table. "You've got to be more careful when you dip your chip—you've got guacamole all over the new T-shirt we just screen printed for you at the studio!"

Grace, who mostly goes by Gracie, looks down at the Hanes T-shirt she spruced up with a Green Day logo and shrugs. Normally staining a cool new shirt like this would bum her out, but not tonight. Tonight she is way too excited to be bummed. And not just because it's taco night at the Alexander-Cline house and her mimi makes the *best* tacos.

Tonight is extra special because it's finally happening— her friends have agreed to get started on creating a fashion business together. Gracie has been wanting to do this with her new besties from Passion for Fashion class for a while now. It all started when her pal Maya Alvarez's hometown in Texas was hit with a horrible hurricane. The girls felt terrible for Maya and her friends and family back in Houston and decided they would help them out by hosting a charity fashion show. The fashion show wound up being a smash hit—they raised $10,000 and were even able to give some of the money to Gracie's mama after her shop, Zoey's Closet, got flooded. Beyond the great feeling of giving back, Gracie had fun working so closely with her friends on a big project like that.

Over the summer, it felt like the fashion show gave her and her P4F friends a reason to be together all the time. As someone who never really had a friend group before, Gracie soaked up every minute of it. But ever since the school year started, things have changed. Because her friends have extracurriculars at their own schools, there isn't much time for hanging out outside of their weekly P4F classes and Shabbat dinners. And even then, getting all five girls together for P4F or Shabbat has become increasingly difficult. Someone always seems to have something more important going on. Gracie has been trying her best to be understanding, but she would be lying if she said she didn't miss hanging out as much as they did when they were working on the fashion show.

That's when it dawned on her: *What if we had a new reason to hang out as much as we used to? We should start a business!* As the only one with no other extracurriculars, Gracie figures she would probably have to do most of the work. But if the P4F girls are as pumped about the idea as she is, she hopes they will naturally wind up collaborating the way they did for the fashion show.

When Gracie first floated the idea during Shabbat at Sophia Ito's house awhile back, everyone liked it, but Ava Morris asked if they could postpone getting started on anything until after fall break when her schedule would lighten a bit. Gracie purposely made sure not to bring it up again—if they were going to do this, she wanted to make sure her friends were fully on board. She didn't want them feeling forced into something they were not truly excited about. So, she patiently waited.

Then last night at Maya's house as the girls were having dinner, Ava finally said her schedule was starting to clear up a bit. And Maya was the one who asked if they could now give more thought to Gracie's idea. The girls all agreed—it was time. From there, they launched into planning mode. First things first, they decided to scrap the idea of an online store and instead promote their designs on TikTok and Instagram, and sell them at Zoey's Closet. This way, they wouldn't have to deal with complicated shipments or anything like that.

Gracie just has one thing left to do before it all becomes official: ask her moms if they're okay with the plan. And what better time to do that than taco night?

Gracie clears her throat and looks around the dinner table as her mama, her mimi, and her little brother, Max, quiet down.

"So, um, I kind of wanted to talk to you all about something," Gracie begins, nervously twirling a strand of her pink hair. She's usually comfortable talking to her moms about anything. But the business idea hinges on her mama being okay with the girls selling out of her store, and Gracie wants to make sure she gets this pitch exactly right.

"What's up, Gracie Girl?" her mimi asks as she places a dollop of sour cream on top of her taco.

"Yeah, honey, you seem tense," her mama chimes in, gently rubbing Gracie's shoulder from where she's seated in the chair next to her. "Everything okay?"

"Well, it's not really that I'm tense," Gracie explains. "It's more that I'm excited. And I hope you both will be as excited as I am about this . . ."

"About what?" Max asks, shoveling a stacked nacho into his mouth. "You're really building the suspense here!"

Gracie takes a deep breath. "Last night at Maya's, the girls and I decided we want to start our own business!" she exclaims. "I had the idea awhile back and everyone loved it, but the timing wasn't quite right. Now it looks like all our schedules have cleared up and it could finally be the perfect time."

"Hmm," her mimi says, nodding her head in consideration. "What kind of business are you thinking?"

"Originally, I was thinking an online store for all of our designs," Gracie shares. "But then last night we realized that might get complicated with shipments and stuff."

"Wow," her mama says, an impressed smile breaking across her face. "You girls have really thought this through."

"Have they?" Max asks, one eyebrow skeptically raised. "Where are you going to sell your stuff if you're not selling it online?"

"Whoa, let's watch it with the critical tone, mister," their mimi says, playfully wagging a finger at Max. "Your sister is clearly excited about this."

"Sorry," Max says to Gracie, his cheeks a little red. "I think I've been watching too much *Shark Tank* with Mama lately."

"We do watch a lot of *Shark Tank*," their mama says with a chuckle. "Anyway, Gracie, Max brings up a fair point. Where do you want to sell your designs?"

"We've got it all figured out," Gracie says, proud of how thoroughly she and her friends thought this idea through already. "We were hoping we would design our own creations, promote them on social media, then sell them at Zoey's Closet. What do you think?"

Gracie waits nervously as her moms silently exchange some imperceptible glances across the table.

"Sounds like a big idea, Gracie!" her mimi finally says. "But if anyone can do it, it's you. What you all did for Maya's hometown was amazing, and I am sure with a lot of hard work you can at least launch this idea."

"And I am happy to support you girls in any way I can," Gracie's mama adds. "Beyond just using Zoey's Closet as the storefront, we can devote some Passion for Fashion classes to creating the designs."

"But, honey," her mimi interjects, "are you sure you know what you're getting yourself into? Owning a business takes a lot of grit and determination. I am all for big ideas, but I also want you to have fun! You're only in middle school. You have the rest of your life for business . . . Of course, I do understand how starting another project with your friends sounds enticing, especially after the success of the fashion show."

"We can handle it, Mimi. I promise," Gracie pleads. "Especially me! Listen, all my friends have other extracurriculars they do, but fashion is my *only* thing. I know I can give my all to this."

"Okay, sweetie," her mama says. "Your mimi and I just want to make sure you're prioritizing being a kid. Starting a business builds character and adds discipline to your life, but at your age, I worry you should just be focused on school and crushes and having a good time."

"Mama, I'll still have time for crushes!" Gracie laughs. Her mind immediately flashes to Ali Mansourian. Ali was Gracie's secret crush for years—though that is no longer much of a secret anymore. She told her P4F friends about him at a paint party at her house over the summer, then he came as her guest to the fashion show. Since then, Gracie and Ali have become really good friends. They are definitely not boyfriend/girlfriend—which is not allowed at her age right now anyway—but it's fun to have a friend!

"Ali and I have actually been hanging out a lot," Gracie tells her family as she helps herself to a third taco. "Having a friend makes school so much easier."

"I'm so happy, hon," her mimi says with a smile. "Between your new life at school and your new business, it sounds like this is going to be your year."

"I really think it might be," Gracie says, a hopeful smile forming on her face.

The truth is, things have been going well for Gracie ever since her mama convinced her to join Passion for Fashion classes over the summer. It was there that Gracie found the group of friends she had always longed for—there's Sophia Ito, the incredible hip-hop dancer with an edgy, preppy style; Ava Morris, the overachiever with an eye for chic, modern looks; Maya Alvarez, the proud Texan with a knack for pairing pretty much anything with her signature cowboy boots; and Lily Smith, the shy New York transplant with the crispest collection of simple, classic looks.

Gracie would have never crossed paths with these girls if it weren't for their shared love of fashion. None of them go to her school or even live particularly close to her house in Ardmore. But despite their different styles and personalities, Gracie and her P4F friends clicked from the moment they met. And spending time with them has caused a big shift in Gracie's life as a whole. It was those girls who started encouraging her to talk to Ali more, and now he's turned into one of her closest friends.

Gracie grabs a helping of nachos and places them on her plate as she considers everything that's changed over the past few months. *If someone told me at the beginning of the summer that I would be starting a business with my best friends and that I would be spending my school days hanging with Ali Mansourian, I don't think I would have believed them*, she thought to herself.

two

"All right, class," Mrs. Shapiro, Gracie's math teacher, announces. "Now don't forget we have a test on the percentages coming up this Wednesday!"

Gracie notes the test reminder down in her iPad with the patchwork cover she sewed at Zoey's Closet over the summer and gets back to staring at the clock. School has never really been Gracie's thing. She mostly spends her class time looking around the room and imagining ways she would spruce it up.

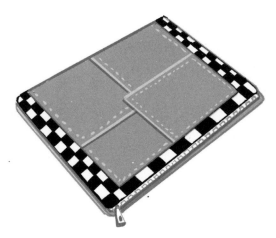

Take Mrs. Shapiro's classroom, for example. It's as simple as a public school classroom could possibly get: whiteboard at the front of the class with an analog clock ticking above it, an American flag hanging above the teacher's desk, and a map and a few colorful posters displayed on the drab cream walls. Gracie would start by changing the walls. She knows the classroom doesn't necessarily have to be as punk as she is, but would it hurt to give them at least *some* color? Maybe a light blue? And why not let the students make some fun desk covers to adorn the boring plasticky wood? *I guess a desk cover would be tricky to write on top of,* Gracie muses. *I wonder if we could come up with a good solution for that for the business . . .*

She's still musing about different ways to create some sort of desk sleeve when the bell rings and snaps her out of it.

"Wanna walk home together?" Ali asks, tapping Gracie on the shoulder from where he sits behind her. "I don't have newspaper today."

"Sure," Gracie says, grabbing her pink-and-black checkered backpack from the floor.

Walking home together has become sort of a ritual for Gracie and Ali whenever he doesn't have to go to meetings for the school newspaper. They have three classes together, including math for their last period, so Ali will usually tap Gracie on the shoulder and snap her out of her daydream right as the bell rings, then he'll ask her to walk. The first time Ali tapped her shoulder, Gracie was so excited she thought her heart was going to jump right out of her chest and onto her desk. She was nervous for the whole walk and barely spoke two words, then immediately rushed inside her house to tell her mimi what had happened.

But now she's gotten used to it. She *definitely* still has a crush on Ali. But he's also a friend who she genuinely enjoys spending time with and feels like she can be herself around.

Gracie deeply inhales the crisp fall air and looks down as her combat boots crunch the brown leaves beneath them. She knows it's more basic than punk rock to admit this, but fall really is her favorite time of the year. The cozy sweaters and cool air have always made it great. Now throw walks with her crush into the mix, and she can't think of a way the season could possibly get any better.

"I like your outfit today," Ali says as they walk toward their neighborhood. "Did you make the dress yourself?"

Gracie looks down at the chunky black sweater dress she spent hours embroidering with tiny silver skulls and stars.

"Sort of," she says. "My mama knitted me the dress for my birthday last year. Then this summer, I thought I would spice it up with the embroidery. Finding the right shoes to pair with it was the tricky part."

"I'm not a big fashion guy, but I would say you nailed it," Ali says, flashing her a heart-melting smile. "I don't think I've ever seen pink combat boots before."

"You probably haven't," Gracie says with a laugh, glancing down at her patent leather bubblegum-pink boots that almost perfectly match her hair color. "These took me *forever* to find. I had to go to so many different vintage stores before I finally found the perfect ones."

"You should join the paper with me," Ali tells her. "I don't want to keep bugging you about it—I know you're busy. But it would be awesome to have you writing the fashion column for us."

"I do like writing," Gracie says. "English is the only class I don't *totally* zone out in. But I like to focus all my attention on one thing. And fashion is my thing right now. Did I tell you me and the P4F girls are starting a business?"

"No way!" Ali exclaims. "That's sweet! What kind of business?"

"We're going to make different fashion designs, then promote them on social media and sell at my mama's studio!" Gracie nervously eyes Ali. She hopes he likes the idea as much as she does.

"That might be the best thing I have ever heard," he says, a giant smile breaking across his face. "No wonder you can't join the paper. You've got a *business* to run."

Gracie giggles. "Well, not quite running it yet, but I'm hoping to be running one soon enough."

"So, what's the plan?" Ali asks. "When are you and the girls going to get everything started?"

"Um, we haven't really fully talked about that since last week, but I'm assuming we'll pick the conversation back up at P4F on Thursday."

"Cool. Have you decided what's going to make the P4F fashion line different from other stuff that's out there?" Ali asks, before adding with a smile, "You know, aside from the fact that you're one of the designers and you're awesome."

"Hmm . . . I *know* it's going to be unique," Gracie says. "But we haven't really talked about exactly how yet."

Gracie swallows hard. She was so excited to get started that she didn't think about how much there is still left to get started on.

When she gets home, her mimi is making chili on the stove and Max is doing some homework at the kitchen table.

"You hungry, sweetie?" her mimi asks. "This chili needs another hour or so, but I've got some apples and peanut butter for you to snack on in the fridge."

"Not really hungry," Gracie says, pulling up a seat next to Max. "I was just walking home with Ali and we were discussing the business. I didn't realize how much we still need to figure out."

"Like what?" Max asks, looking up from his homework. "You seemed like you had things pretty figured out at dinner."

"Yeah," Gracie sighs. "But what's going to make our brand different? That's something I haven't discussed with the girls yet. And when are we going to work on things?"

"Now this is not *my* business," her mimi says, the delicious smell of the chili wafting around the kitchen as she gives it a stir, "but, as an outsider looking in, I would say you girls should try to infuse your individuality into the line as much as you can. You're all so different—it would be incredible to get all of those personalities into one fashion line."

Something clicks in her mind. "Mimi, you're a *genius*," Gracie says, jumping out of her seat and running upstairs to her room. As soon as she plops on her bed, Gracie grabs her phone and pulls up the P4F group text.

Lily
Sure! I'm free whenever. Not meeting with the rabbi until tomorrow.

Maya
So exciting! I could chat in an hour. At the parish right now.

Ava
Can we do around 7? I've got violin then tutoring. So busy 😩

Sophia
I'm just walking into hip-hop now, then my mom said we're having family dinner at 7 and she's super intense about us all eating dinner at the table together without phones. Maybe after dinner?

My moms don't usually like me being on the phone after 8 😞

Lily
Gracie, why don't we just chat right now and fill the rest of the girls in on Thursday at P4F?

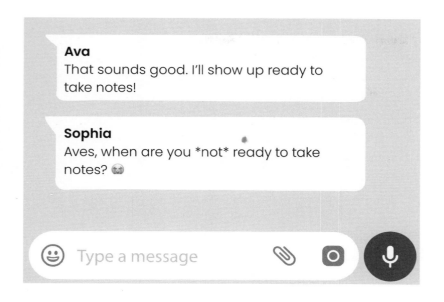

Gracie giggles. It's true. Even in their Passion for Fashion classes, Ava is always the most diligent student, carefully jotting down all of Gracie's mama's instructions in a notebook.

Before Gracie knows it, her phone is ringing and Lily's name is populating the screen. Gracie perks up at the increasingly familiar sight. Ever since the school year started, it feels like Lily is the only P4F girl who still has time for her. Gracie knows she doesn't show it often, but she appreciates that her friend is always the first to call or say yes to a hangout—no matter how busy her schedule gets with soccer and her cantor's class.

"Lily," Gracie says as she answers. "I am *so* excited to tell you this idea."

"Tell me!" Lily begs, her soft voice going up one teensy octave. "I can't wait to hear."

"Okay, so, I was walking home with Ali today," Gracie says, instantly appreciating the fact that her friend doesn't freak out over the mention of her crush's name. "And I was telling him about our business idea and he started asking me all these questions, like what makes our brand unique."

"Huh," Lily says thoughtfully, considering the question. "What did you say?"

"Well, that was the problem," Gracie says. "I was stumped. So, I went home and talked it out with my mimi, and she pointed out how different we all are."

"I think I know where you're going with this and I already like it," Lily says, a gentle smile breaking across her face. "It would be so fun to draw from our different backgrounds. I've been putting together a 'minimalist '90s looks' Pinterest board I could draw inspo from for my designs."

"Right!" Gracie exclaims. "The whole point would be to highlight our individual styles while bringing us together at the same time. Like, maybe one collection is all finger knitted scarves. Or another is desk sleeves."

"Desk sleeves?" Lily asks, her blond brows lightly furrowed "What are those?"

"Just an idea I was thinking about while I was zoning out in class today," Gracie says. "Don't you think it would be so cool to have a way to spice up our desktops?"

"Oh," Lily says. "I see what you mean. Like a book sleeve, but for our desks?"

"*Exactly*," Gracie says. "Anyway, I'm still workshopping that idea, but the point is, whatever we make, we can each make one type of item with our own twist on it. So it all feels like it's one line, but it still shows off our different styles. Like, we could do beanies. And each of us could design a beanie that references our own personal fashion. Mine will *obviously* have a punk flair. But Ava could do something girly. And Maya could draw on her Texas roots for inspiration, and maybe Sophia could even pick up on some street style while she's in New York this weekend."

"Totally." Lily nods. "I really like this. I'm sure the girls are going to be so excited when we tell them at P4F."

Gracie feels a nervous bubble growing at the pit of her stomach. "Hey, Lily?" she asks. "Do you think they're as excited about this as we are?"

"Yes!" Lily reassures. "Why wouldn't they be?"

"I don't know." Gracie shrugs. "It just seems like they weren't super excited to v-chat about it tonight."

"Everyone's schedules are packed," Lily says. "But that doesn't mean they're not excited."

"Yeah, I guess that's true," Gracie says with a nod. "Thanks. I needed to hear that."

"Any time," Lily says with a smile. "I have to go do some prep for my cantor's class tomorrow, but call me if you have any more ideas, okay?"

"Okay!" Gracie agrees before hanging up.

She feels silly for even asking Lily the question. *Of course they're excited*, she tells herself. *Maya was the one who brought up the business at Shabbat! Not you. They're just a little busy right now, that's all.*

Gracie whips out a sketchbook from under her bed and starts doodling some ideas for the business. *This is why I can't be on the school newspaper*, she tells herself. *If everyone else is busy, I need to be extra focused on the business!*

three

"Gracie!" Ali calls out from down the hallway at school. "Wait up!"

Gracie pauses by the hall door, her heart doing a couple tiny somersaults as Ali jogs over to her. Ali may be her friend now, but the fact that he's shouting her name down the hall is still absolutely, positively *thrilling*.

"Newspaper got canceled today," he says, slightly winded. "Wanna walk home together?"

"Sure," Gracie says, her lips curving upward into a shy smile. "Want to take the long way home? It's so nice out."

"I'm down." Ali holds the door open as Gracie makes her way out of school into the perfect fall day. "*Anything* to put off starting that history paper."

"You still haven't started?" Gracie asks, her eyes wide. "My moms made me start that last week!"

"I *wish* I started last week," Ali says with a sigh. "I always do this. I leave my projects to the last minute and then I get so nervous the day before an assignment is due."

"I do that sometimes too," Gracie says. "Especially with this business I'm trying to start. I keep feeling like I would rather be focusing my attention on that than on boring old *homework*, you know?"

"Yeah," Ali says with a nod. "How's the business coming along anyway?"

"Well, actually, not to call you out, but I sort of freaked out after we talked about it on Monday," Gracie says with a nervous chuckle. "I realized how much we still hadn't figured out."

"Oh no!" Ali frowns, the dangly clip-on earring he has in his right ear poking out from behind his shaggy black hair as he thrusts his head into his palm. "I wasn't trying to stress you out. The business seems awesome! I was just asking questions because I was curious about it."

"No, it actually wound up being a good thing," Gracie says with a reassuring smile. "You got me thinking about what makes our business unique."

". . . and?" Ali asks. "What's the answer?"

"I'm glad you asked," Gracie says, a proud smile busting across her face. "The answer is, all of us. My P4F friends and I are all very different. And I'm thinking if we each make a version of every item with our own special twist, this brand will be unlike anything anyone has ever seen."

"All right!" Ali says, clapping his hands. "This sounds sick."

"Thanks," Gracie says. She could feel her face growing warm. She's sure it must be the same pink shade as her hair. "I'm super excited about it."

"You should be," Ali says as he turns toward their street. "Oh! By the way, I almost forgot to ask. Sue Ellen, who runs the fashion section at the paper, suggested we feature you as the best dressed in our class for the next paper. Would you be into that?"

"Are you serious?!" Gracie exclaims, fighting the urge to do victory cartwheels down the block. *Play it cool, Gracie. Play it cool! Ah, forget it.* "Ali, this is, like, a dream come true! No offense to all the music articles you write, but the minute the student newspaper comes out, I skip *straight* to the Best Dressed feature."

"It's okay," Ali says with a shrug. "I get it. The Best Dressed feature is a newspaper staple. Did you know they've been doing it since the '60s?"

"Yep," Gracie says, beaming. "My Grandma Zoey, the one who my mama named Zoey's Closet after, actually got a feature in it when she was in middle school."

"No way!" Ali looks impressed. "That's amazing! Maybe we could show your features side by side. I would have to poke around in the archives, but I'm sure I could find it."

"You don't have to!" Gracie says. "My mama has a copy of it somewhere around the house. I'll just have her find it."

"Great," Ali says, pulling out his phone. "I'm texting Sue Ellen right now. She's going to be so hyped that you're in."

Gracie cannot believe it. Of course, fashion has always meant a lot to her. But she knows her personal sense of style isn't exactly for everyone. When she first dyed her hair pink last year, she heard the not-so-nice whispers from some of the kids in her class. Just today, when she showed up to school in a black jean skirt paired with a white tee and black denim vest—she spent hours adorning it with studs on the collar and pink patches featuring little odes to her favorite bands—she couldn't help but notice some funny looks from her peers.

Mabel Jones even tapped on her shoulder during science class today to ask if the studs she so carefully picked out "hurt." When Gracie told her they didn't, Mabel just sort of looked at her with an icked-out expression on her face and said, "They look kind of creepy."

Gracie didn't really mind the hate. If anything, she welcomed it. A look wouldn't truly be punk if everyone got it. But the fact that someone as cool as Sue Ellen LePage, the fashion editor for the *Ardmore Aardvark Gazette*, who consistently dresses like she belongs in a New York street style blog, respects Gracie's style choices really means a lot.

"So, what do I have to do to prepare?" Gracie asks Ali. "You know, aside from prepping the outfits."

"That should mostly be it," Ali says. "You know how it works. We basically track your outfits for a whole week. We'll probably start next Monday. Poppy, the photographer for the paper, will take your picture in the morning and Sue Ellen will ask you questions about your outfit over lunch."

"This sounds awesome," Gracie says, her mind already buzzing with outfit ideas. "I can't wait."

When Gracie gets home, she practically bursts through the door. "Mimi! Max!" she shouts. "Anyone home? I have some major news!"

"Hi, sweetie," her mama says, rushing down the stairs. "What's going on? Mimi took Max to Little League."

"Mama?" Gracie asks, a little surprised. "What are you doing home right now? Shouldn't you be at Zoey's Closet?"

"The studio was empty and I wasn't teaching any classes this afternoon, so I figured I'd close up shop and head home early," her mama says with a shrug. "Anyway, hon, what's all the excitement about?"

"Get this," Gracie says, taking a deep breath before sharing the news. "I was walking home with Ali today and he says Sue Ellen, the supercool eighth grader who runs the fashion section of the *Ardmore Aardvark Gazette*, wants to feature me as their best dressed student for this month's paper. Me! Just like Grandma Zoey!"

"Oh, Gracie Girl," her mama says, her eyes welling up. "This is so special. She would have been so proud."

"I know," Gracie says, her heart immediately warming. "Do you have the original copy of when she was featured saved? I remember it was somewhere at Zoey's Closet, but did it get messed up in the flood?"

"Well, it would have," her mama says, a sad look washing over her face as she thinks about the flood that hit her studio a few months ago. "But luckily, it's one of my most prized possessions, so I actually had it in our floodproof safe. It's in the attic now. Want me to grab it for you?"

"That would be awesome," Gracie says. "I was telling Ali how Grandma Zoey also was chosen as best dressed, and he said it would be cool if we could run our features side by side."

"That is such a great idea!" her mama exclaims, beaming. "You kids are so thoughtful and creative. I'll go grab that feature and get it to you in a minute."

"Sounds good," Gracie says, making her way up to her room. "I should tell all the P4F girls about this."

"Yes," her mama says, giving her a kiss on top of her head. "They are going to be so happy for you!"

As soon as Gracie gets to her room, she pulls up the group text on her phone.

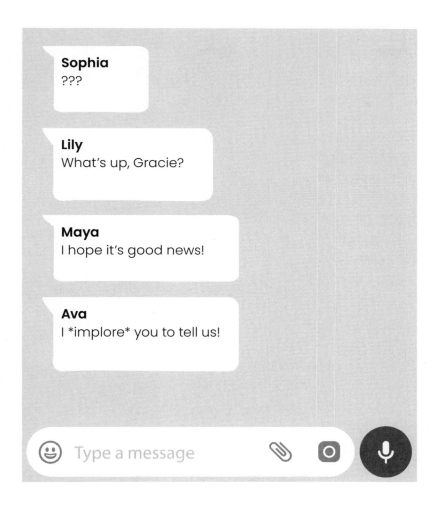

Gracie lets out a laugh at Ava's text. Her friend has been casually inserting big words into conversation for weeks now to prep for the vocabulary section of the high school entrance exams.

I just found out I was chosen to be this month's best dressed student in the school newspaper!

Lily
Best dressed? So cool!

Sophia
Freaking out for you!!!!!

Ava
What an awe-inspiring accomplishment. You're going down in your school's history! So proud!

Thanks! I'm so excited. Going to spend the next few hours thinking about the business, but then I've gotta get to outfit planning . . .

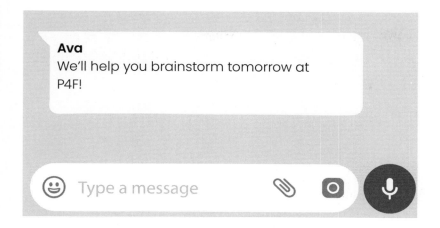

Gracie puts her phone down and takes a deep breath. *As cool as this is, I can't let this distract me,* she tells herself. *The business has to come first.*

"Gracie," her mama says as she knocks from the other side of the door. "I found the article." She comes in and sits at the foot of Gracie's bed, the article carefully held in her hand.

"Wow," Gracie says, peering over her shoulder. "I know I've seen this before, but I just can't get over how Grandma Zoey was, like, *shockingly* cool."

"She really was," her mama says with a laugh. "And you know, she made most of her own outfits herself, just like you."

"So cool," Gracie says, scanning the pictures of her grandma rocking wide bell bottoms with cool patterns and flowy jumpsuits paired with giant sunglasses. "She looks like a celebrity!"

"Maybe one day your grandchild will be looking at your feature thinking *you* look like a celebrity," her mama says, with a proud smile. "You know, you remind me a lot of her."

"I wish I knew her better," Gracie says, her heart sinking as she thinks about what little time she got to spend with her late grandma. "She seemed so awesome."

"She was," her mama says. "But we have her memories— and those will carry on in our hearts and our minds forever."

"That's true," Gracie says, still gazing at the pictures. "You know, I bet the girls and I could get some inspiration for the business from these old pictures. What if we each made a '70s-inspired look?"

"That's a great idea," her mama says, getting up. "I'll let you get back to brainstorming. But before I go, I have some exciting news for you . . ." She pauses and says with a dramatic flourish, "We're going away to the Poconos next weekend!"

Gracie looks blankly back at her mama. "What?" Gracie asks, confused. "Didn't you and Mimi rent out the cabin for all of fall?"

"Yes, but the family who was supposed to be staying there this weekend just canceled," her mama explains. "Mimi and I thought we might as well take advantage and head up there for a little getaway."

Gracie feels torn. Normally, this would be great news. The Poconos is one of her favorite places on the entire planet! But she has so much going on here right now. The girls have all been so busy during the weekdays, so Gracie was hoping that they could spend their weekends really ironing out the business. But a weekend in the Poconos would mean a weekend of total isolation with no Wi-Fi. Definitely no collaborating with the P4F girls from there.

"Do you think I could bring the girls?" Gracie asks, perking up at the idea. "That way we could work on the business while we're there!"

"I wish you could bring them all, honey," her mama says. "We just don't have room for four extra guests in our cabin. But you know, I'm sure you could bring one friend."

"Deal," Gracie says. "I know exactly who I'll bring."

"Good," her mama says with a smile. "This will be fun!"

As soon as her mama shuts the door, Gracie has Lily on speed dial. What better way to show Lily how much she appreciates her unwavering friendship than an invite to Gracie's favorite place on earth?

"Hello?" Lily answers, her soft voice barely projecting from the other line.

"Lil!" Gracie booms. "Super exciting news—my mama just told me we're going to the Poconos this weekend and I could bring a friend! Would you want to come?"

"Wait, this sounds so fun!" Lily says, her voice picking up some energy. "I am so in."

"Awesome," Gracie says. "It's the best place ever. You're going to love it. I can't wait to show you everything."

"I've never been," Lily says. "But my dad went once and said it was beautiful."

"It really is," Gracie says. "I'm bummed we don't have room for all the P4F girls, but I figure you and I could get a lot of business planning done for everyone while we're away."

"Definitely," Lily confirms. "Okay, I'm going to run downstairs and ask my dad, but I'm sure he'll be fine with it. I'll text you what he says!"

"Sounds good," Gracie says, hanging up.

Ten seconds later, Gracie's phone lights up with a text from Lily: *He said I can go! Yay!* 😊

four

Gracie looks down at her phone to check the time: 6:05 p.m. *Ugh. They're late.*

"Did any of them tell you they were going to be late?" Gracie asks Lily, who's seated on the chrome stool across the table from her. "We purposely picked this time because it worked with all of their busy schedules!"

"No," Lily quietly replies, an undeniable look of pity making its way across her face. "But it's only been five minutes. I'm sure they will be here soon."

Gracie was so excited for Passion for Fashion class today that she came to Zoey's Closet right after school. In fact, Ali asked to walk with her, and Gracie said no because she wanted to come straight here! *That* was how excited she was—she bailed on a walk with her crush to get here early.

Of course, by the time she got here it was only three thirty, and the girls purposely scheduled Passion for Fashion for six o'clock on Thursdays so that everyone could make it there after their other extracurriculars. But Gracie just loves being at Zoey's Closet. When her mama refurbished it after the flood, she let Gracie have a large say in what the new design was going to be like. It was Gracie who chose the sparkly pink linoleum floor and the fuzzy white benches by the windows.

But her mama is the real creative genius. She's the one who decided to do just one large white table in the center of the room, instead of a bunch of tables that would make the store look cluttered. And she's the one who said that the fuzzy benches Gracie picked out should probably have some storage space inside of them to store fashion magazines. Now they call it the Inspiration Station. But the sewing machines were Gracie's passion project. Yes, her mama is the one who puff painted each of the P4F girls' names onto the sewing machines. But it was Gracie who came up with the idea and even picked out which colors they would use for each of her friends. Zoey's Closet has always felt like home to her, but it's important to Gracie that her P4F friends feel that same sense of ease and comfort here.

Like today, for example. When she was done with her homework, Gracie decided she would take the lead on ordering dinner for her friends to munch on during P4F class. She figured they would be hungry after their various activities, and she wanted to make sure there would be food that her friends would want to eat. So, she ordered from the new fast casual place that just opened down the street— salmon for Ava because it's "brain food" and Ava is intense about getting her brain into tip-top shape, a taco salad for Sophia because she says she's always craving good Mexican food when she's scarfing down Italian on the weekends with her dad in New York, a pulled pork bowl for Maya who misses the Texan flavors she left behind in her hometown, and rice and chicken for Lily who likes to keep her food like her style: simple. Her friends may be busy with their extracurriculars, but helping her mama make sure Passion for Fashion is as great as it could possibly be feels like an *extra* extracurricular for Gracie.

Plus, today's class is special. It's the first time they're going to be discussing the new business!

She looks down at her phone again: 6:07 p.m.

"Maybe you girls should try giving them a call," her mama suggests from across the table, sensing Gracie's unease. "Just to get an idea of when they'll be here."

"Good idea, Ms. Anna," Lily says to Gracie's mama with a calm smile. "Gracie, do you want to call or should I?"

"Maybe we should just text," Gracie says. "That's easier. I'll send something now."

TODAY

Hey, are you all still coming today?

Ava
I was just amidst texting you.
Unfortunately I'm not going to make it. Still
with my French tutor. 😣 My MOST sincere
apologies! Sophia already promised she
would take notes to avail me.

Sophia
Sorry, wanted to make sure I nailed my
dance routine before we left the house.
But I've got it down and am OMW! Should
be there soon.

Maya
The club I started at school was a way
bigger hit than expected! Just left school,
heading over now!

 Type a message

Gracie sighs. She was hoping the business might make P4F activities more of a priority for her friends, but it seems like they're flaking just as much as they were before they've even started. It's not that she has anything against her friends being excited about their other extracurriculars. She just wishes this was their main priority, the way it is for her.

"Mama, you can give Ava's salmon to the unhoused person down the street," Gracie says. "It looks like she's not coming."

"Oh, that's too bad that she can't make it," her mama says. "What does she have going on?"

"She's still with her French tutor," Gracie says. "Lily, do you think we should talk about the business without her? I don't really want to hold off a whole other week."

"We might as well," Lily says. "She said Sophia will be taking notes for her anyway . . ."

"I'm here! I'm here!" Lily's reasoning is interrupted by Sophia breathlessly running through the door. "Ms. Anna, I'm so sorry I'm late."

"Don't worry about it, sweetie," Gracie's mama says. "You want some taco salad?"

"That sounds great!" Sophia says, taking off the bright blue Adidas track jacket she has on with matching pants and a white tank. "Oof, I really worked up a sweat today."

"Hey, Soph," Gracie says before Lily echoes, "Hi, Sophia."

"Hi, girls," Sophia says with a smile as she settles into the seat next to Lily. "I'm so sorry I'm late to business brainstorming. But I'm here and I'm ready! I even brought a notebook and pen for Ava."

She isn't kidding. Gracie watches as Sophia takes a pocket-sized silver notebook and sparkly pink gel pen out of her track pants.

Gracie clears her throat. "We should probably wait until Maya—"

"Hi, y'all!" Maya shouts as she walks through the door. "Sorry, I started a country music club at school and I thought I would be the only member, but it turns out there are tons of country music fans at my school! We wound up staying a whole extra hour discussing our favorite songs by Kacey Musgraves and The Chicks."

"No worries," Sophia says, taking a large bite out of her taco salad. "Gracie was just about to start telling us her idea for the business."

"Oh! Amazing," Maya says with a big smile as she takes a seat at her sewing machine next to Sophia's. "What are you thinking, Gracie?"

"Before you girls start talking shop, Maya, can I get you a pulled pork bowl?" Gracie's mama asks. "Gracie ordered one for you from the new fast casual place that just opened up down the street."

"Pulled pork?" Maya asks, a jolt of excitement visibly making its way up her spine. "I haven't had good pulled pork since I was in Texas!"

"Yeah, I remembered you said that," Gracie says. "I ordered it for you as soon as I saw it on the menu."

"She did that for all of us," Lily adds. "She got me chicken and rice because she knows I like to keep it simple."

"Wait, did you get me the taco salad because I mentioned missing Mexican food in New York?" Sophia asks.

"Yep," Gracie says with a smile. "I figured you might appreciate it."

"I *really* do," Sophia says, taking another large bite of her salad. "Thanks, Gracie."

"Of course," Gracie says, a proud smile making its way across her face. They may be late, but at least they appreciate everything she does.

"So," Maya says, taking a bite out of her pulled pork bowl. "Tell us what you've been thinking for the business!"

"Yes," Sophia says, opening her notebook and taking the cap off her pen. "I'm ready."

"Okay, here it goes," Gracie begins. "So, I was walking home from school with Ali the other day and he was asking what makes our business different. To be honest, the question kind of stumped me, but then my mimi helped me realize: it's *us*! Each of us have a unique sense of style. Like, Maya, look at your outfit today. You've paired that chunky beige sweater with a slip skirt, but it's not just *any* old slip skirt. It's a red paisley one that gives it your signature country flair."

"And that's the whole idea," Lily cuts in, still as quiet as ever but more excited. "We would each take a piece of clothing, like a slip skirt, and then do our own take on the design."

"Oh my gosh!" Maya says, clapping her hands excitedly. "This is genius! And we could give each style a name after one of us."

"Totally!" Gracie exclaims, a sense of relief washing over her as she sees her friends are as enthusiastic about this as she is. "Like, the country look you design could be 'The Maya.'"

"I can't *wait* to get these notes to Ava," Sophia says, scribbling away. "She is going to love this."

"And I'm here to guide you girls throughout the creation process," Gracie's mama adds. "So, today I was thinking we could start on your first product. Something simple. Maybe a finger knitted scarf?"

"Simple would probably be best for Ava," Sophia says, still jotting everything down. "I don't want her to have to catch up on something super complex when she comes to P4F next week."

"Wonderful," Gracie's mama says, getting up to grab the box of yarn from the supply closet. When she returns, she simply dumps the many brightly colorful balls of yarn onto the table. "I don't think you girls will need much instruction here. After all, this was what our first class was on. But let me know if you need any assistance."

"It's a bummer Ava can't be here," Gracie laments, taking one last bite of her buffalo chicken salad before grabbing a black-and-silver ball and weaving the yarn around her fingers. "Is everyone busy this weekend? Maybe we could catch up with her then."

"My parents are hosting a sing-along at the church all day Saturday and I promised them I would help out," Maya says as she picks out a ball made out of what looks more like shredded denim. "But I'm around next weekend to meet then."

"Yeah, this weekend is no good for me either," Sophia says, twisting the neon yellow string through her fingers. "I'm going straight to New York to be with my dad first thing Saturday morning. But I'm staying in Lower Merion the following weekend, so I'm around then too! And I think Ava has a pretty light workload that weekend, so she should be able to hang."

"Perfect!" Maya says happily. "Wow, this will be so fun. A whole weekend of P4F and focusing on the business."

Gracie and Lily look at each other nervously. *Of course* the one weekend everyone is available is the weekend that they are going to be in the Poconos with no service.

Gracie gulps hard. "Um, well, about that," she says before adding super quickly, "Lily and I aren't going to be around next weekend."

"Huh," Sophia says, her brows furrowed. "Where are you going?"

"Ms. Brie and I are taking the family to our cabin in the Poconos," Gracie's mama chimes in, trying to help. "So sorry that it's interrupting your schedule, girls."

"What about you, Lily?" Maya asks. "Where are you going?"

"Um, I'm actually going with them," she says, her voice a near-whisper and her eyes hyper-focused on the lilac scarf she's knitting. "Gracie invited me earlier this week."

"Oh," Sophia says, nodding slowly. "Got it."

"Sorry, girls," Gracie says quickly. "The Poconos is my favorite place ever. I wish I could take you all. It's just . . . it's a small cabin."

"Totally." Maya nods, the smile on her face a little *too* wide. "Makes sense. No hard feelings."

Sophia shrugs. "No biggie."

The girls sit silently for a few awkward seconds that feel more like minutes before Gracie's mama finally cuts in.

"All right, we don't have much time left, but who wants to learn how to turn their scarf into a shawl?" she says, looking at her bright orange rubber watch. "Even if you don't wind up doing it now, it could be a good trick to have up your sleeve."

"Sure," Gracie nods, desperate to change the subject. "That sounds awesome."

five

"Gracie, hon," her mimi says as she drives her Prius up the long, windy driveway to Ava's family's mansion. "Is everything okay?"

Gracie looks down at her clammy hands and isn't quite sure how to answer.

Ever since they started this tradition over the summer, Shabbat Friday has become the day Gracie looks forward to the most every week. The tradition started at one of their very first slumber parties at Lily's house. Lily seemed sort of down that night and when the girls asked why, she revealed that Friday used to be the night when she would celebrate Shabbat with her mom and the Jewish side of her family. While her dad tried to keep the spirit of her Jewish culture alive even after her mom passed away and they moved to Philadelphia, the fact of the matter was it just didn't feel the same. So, the girls stepped in to make a new tradition for their friend. They decided that even though none of them except Lily were Jewish, they could still help her celebrate her cultural tradition by hosting their own version of a weekly Shabbat dinner. Ever since then, the girls have taken turns on Friday hosting Shabbat dinner followed by a slumber party.

Usually, Friday cannot come soon enough. Gracie loves to spend quality time catching up with her friends and taking part in the Jewish tradition that she's come to find so much comfort in. But this week feels different. Things already started off tense in P4F class yesterday with everyone being so caught up in their other extracurriculars, then they got *super* awkward after mentioning the Poconos.

"I don't know," Gracie replies to her mimi. "Things were just so . . . weird in class yesterday."

"Because of the Poconos?" her mimi asks as she parks her car in front of Ava's gigantic home. "I'm sorry we can't invite everyone, honey. There just isn't enough room."

"I know," Gracie says as she nods. "I'm still happy I get to bring Lily. I know we're going to have a great time when we're there. It's just awkward when it's always a group of five of us together, you know?"

"Well, even if they were a little hurt, I'm sure the girls understand."

"I think they do," Gracie says. "When I called Lily about it after school today, she reminded me that everyone has been talking in the group text like normal since last night."

"That's a great sign!" her mimi says. "There would not be group text chatter if things were seriously off. Will everybody be here at Ava's tonight?"

"Everyone was supposed to," Gracie sighs, "but Maya canceled because her parents have a last-minute speaking engagement and she has to stay back and watch her brothers."

"That's too bad," her mimi says. "But it sounds like her family needs her."

"Yeah," Gracie says. "You don't think it's an excuse, do you? Like, she doesn't want to hang out with me after I didn't invite her? All I've wanted for the past few months is for the five of us to hang out as much as we did over the summer, and I feel like I might have just ruined everything with this Poconos situation."

Her mimi lets out a laugh. "Oh, sweetie, no," she says. "I promise this is not as big of a deal to anybody else but you. Now, go in there and have some fun with your friends."

"Okay," Gracie nervously agrees, slowly making her way out of the car. "Let's hope you're right."

"Hey," her mimi calls out a little too loudly before Gracie shuts the door. "You know the best way to make something not awkward?"

"What?" Gracie asks, desperate for any advice on the matter.

"*Don't be awkward.* Just go in there and act like nothing weird happened last night!"

Gracie nods. "Thanks, Mimi."

Don't be awkward. Gracie repeats the advice in her head like a mantra as she lets herself into the Morris home and makes her way to the dining room. This will be easy! These are her best friends. And they've got business to discuss! Without this weekend or the next to work on things, they'll have to spend tonight doing some serious planning. Gracie suddenly feels a pang of relief to have Ava here. If there's one thing Ava is great at, it's getting down to business. Gracie has been trying her best to lead the charge here, but Ava can help them get really organized.

Gracie walks for what feels like a mile before she finally gets to the dining room. Sometimes she still finds herself shocked that she has a friend who lives in a home like this. The first time she came to the Morrises', Gracie knew just based on the neighborhood that the house would be pretty nice. But this house isn't just pretty nice. It's a beautiful giant brick home with white accents, plus a perfectly manicured garden and pool house. Inside the house, there are seven bedrooms, nine bathrooms, a movie theater, an indoor pool, and a home gym. The dining room where Shabbat is typically hosted is one of *three* dining rooms.

This house is wild, Gracie thinks to herself.

When Gracie finally makes her way into the beautiful room with the chandelier hanging above the large mahogany table, she sees three of her friends are already seated.

"Gracie! Hi!" the girls exclaim almost in unison.

Gracie waves back. *Okay, a friendly "hi" has to be a good sign, right?!*

"Gracie, it's great to see you," Mrs. Morris says, Mr. Morris trailing behind her as she makes her way into the dining room from the kitchen. "And look at that outfit!"

Gracie bashfully smiles as she looks down at the green-and-black checkered pants she's paired with a black Ramones T-shirt, black booties, and her black leather jacket. "You like?"

"This probably means nothing coming from a dorky dad," Mr. Morris says, "but you look *very* cool."

Gracie laughs. When she first met them, Gracie was super intimidated by Ava's successful parents. Mr. Morris is a surgeon and Mrs. Morris is a partner at a top Philadelphia law firm. Gracie's parents both work too—her mimi is a painter and her mama owns Zoey's Closet. But while Gracie loves their small home with its colorful walls and cozy details, it's a far cry from this palatial estate. Everything about the Morris family just sort of feels . . . intimidating. Luckily, as she's come to know Ava's parents, Gracie's nerves have eased up. They are both really nice and always welcome Gracie with open arms.

"So, should we get started?" Ava asks as Gracie takes a seat at the dinner table. "I just had an hour of entrance exam tutoring followed by two hours of lacrosse practice. I am *famished.*"

Gracie makes a mental note to hold off until they've eaten

to bring up the business. She wants Ava to be feeling good and ready to focus on this important discussion.

"Yeah, I didn't have hip-hop practice today, but a few of the girls and I met up to practice after school and I majorly worked up an appetite," Sophia chimes in, deeply inhaling before she adds, "Plus, it smells so good in here. What did you cook, Mr. M?"

"I didn't have any surgeries booked, so I decided to spend the day preparing a traditional Jewish meal for you girls," Mr. Morris says, placing a perfectly braised brisket on the table. "We've got it all. Brisket, matzo ball soup, fresh-baked challah, latkes, smoked salmon, and even some gefilte fish, if any of you are feeling adventurous."

"I can't believe you got the gefilte fish," Lily says with a giggle. "It was never my thing, but my mom loved it. She was always trying to get me to try some."

"Aw," said Mrs. Morris, gently giving Lily a rub on the back. "Well, I'm happy we could bring that little memory back for you."

Mr. Morris hands his wife the lighter on the mantle of the fireplace and she quietly lights the two candles they have placed on the table.

"Now, we'll let you girls get to it," she says. "Mr. Morris and I are going to prep dessert in the kitchen."

"Just holler if you need anything!" Mr. Morris tells the girls, giving them a friendly wave before following Mrs. Morris into the kitchen.

Once he makes his way out, the girls go straight into placing their hands over their eyes. When they first started doing this, Gracie actively had to remind herself of what to do and when. But now it feels almost instinctual. They repeat the eye-covering motion three times, then Lily does the Jewish blessing. From there, Gracie knows it's her turn to read "A Friend," by Gillian Jones, the poem they picked at their very first Shabbat dinner. Gracie used to have to read the poem from her phone, but now she knows it by heart.

Once Gracie completes the poem, they dig into their dinner.

"This might be the best kugel I've ever had," Lily says, her eyes wide as she takes a delicate bite. "And that's saying a lot—my mom used to make a *really* good kugel."

"And this matzo ball soup!" Sophia exclaims as she slurps up a spoonful. "It tastes like it was sent down here straight from a kitchen in heaven."

Gracie laughs as she takes a bite of her warm, flaky challah. *Whoa.* Sophia wasn't exaggerating. This food is *incredible.*

"Ava," Gracie says. "Your dad should open a restaurant! This food is unbelievable."

"*Please* don't tell him that," Ava begs with a laugh as she helps herself to a third latke. "He is already incredibly conceited about his cooking. We have to keep him humble."

Gracie eyes the plate of gelatinous-looking fish on the table. It is *definitely* not something she would typically eat. But if she tries it at any point, it should be here when Mr. Morris made it, right?

"Lily, is that the fish thing you were talking about with Mr. Morris?" she asks her friend as she points to the dish.

"Yep." Lily nods. "Gefilte fish. It looks kind of funky, but people really love it. It was my mom's favorite."

"Should I try it?" Gracie asks, curious but a bit nervous.

"Go for it!" Lily says. "It's not for me, but that's mostly just because I don't like the soft texture. The actual flavor is really good."

"I concur." Ava nods as she serves herself some. "I tried some in the kitchen when my dad was prepping it and it didn't taste fishy at all. Exceptionally mild."

"Okay," Gracie says, reaching her plate over to where Ava is seated across from her. "Can you serve me some?"

Ava carefully places some on her plate and Gracie quickly takes a bite.

"Huh," Gracie says, nodding slowly as she lets the new food fill her mouth. "Ava, you're right. This is super mild. If nobody told me this was fish, I wouldn't have even guessed it! And honestly? I kind of like the texture!"

"My mom would have been so happy that I found friends who like gefilte fish," Lily says with a sad smile. "I wish she could have been here to meet you all."

"Me too," Gracie says with a sympathetic nod. She really means it. Lily talks about her mom all the time and she sounds like she was awesome.

By the time they finish eating, Gracie is feeling as good as new. *Mimi was right*, she thinks. *Things are only awkward if you make them awkward.*

"So, Ava, did Sophia catch you up on my idea for the business?" Gracie asks, proud of herself for not rushing the conversation while they were still eating. Self-control can be hard!

"She has," Ava says, nodding. "But I haven't had a chance to read all her notes yet. I'm sorry. My schedule has *never* been more strenuous."

"Uh, I don't know what strenuous means," Gracie says. "But if it means busy, I believe you."

"Strenuous, s-t-r-e-n-u-o-us. Adjective, meaning 'requiring or using great exertion,'" Ava recites as if she's at a spelling bee. "It's one of my vocab words."

"I figured," Gracie says with a giggle. "Well, if you want me to catch you up now so you don't have to read the notes, I can just tell you."

"It's *such* a good idea," Lily adds with a smile. "You're going to love it."

"And we have a lot to do," Gracie says. "I could really use your help getting organized."

"I'm sorry, but can we not talk about business right now?" Sophia groans. "Lily's right. It *is* a really good idea. But I'm already so tired from hip-hop and I have to wake up super early tomorrow to go to New York."

"Yeah, Gracie, I'm sorry, but can this wait maybe even just until tomorrow morning?" Ava asks. "I know I nailed that strenuous definition, but my brain is *fried* right now. I just want to chill the rest of the night."

Lily softly mouths, *Sorry*, to Gracie from across the table.

"That's okay," Gracie says as she tries to plaster on a smile. "No big deal. Why don't we just . . . watch a movie?"

"*Great* idea," Ava says. "I'll cue up *Clueless* in the theater."

Gracie tries her best to swallow her disappointment. This was supposed to be the night they were all finally going to be together to discuss the business. But what can she do if nobody feels like discussing? She can't force them.

Don't make it awkward, she reminds herself. *After all, wasn't the point of the business to spend more time with your friends? Don't ruin the time you do have with them by being mad. Just pretend like it's fine and enjoy the movie.*

SIX

Gracie takes one last look at her outfit in the mirror before deciding to phone Lily for a consultation.

"Hello?" Lily answers the FaceTime from bed, her eyes still partially shut. "Gracie? What time is it?"

"Yeah, sorry about the early call," Gracie says, though she needs her friend too badly right now to be *super* sorry. "It's six thirty. I've been up since five. Today's the big day!"

"Oh yeah, your feature!" Lily says, the revelation jolting her upright. "How could I forget?"

"To be fair, you might have remembered when you naturally woke up," Gracie says with a smile. "I did just rudely call you an hour earlier than you normally would get up for school."

Lily nods. "Good point. But enough about my sleep schedule. Have you settled on your Day One look?"

Gracie knows the business needs her now more than ever, but she has to admit this *Ardmore Aardvark Gazette* feature kind of wound up taking over her entire weekend. By last night, she finally narrowed down the five looks she plans to rock throughout the week. But deciding which of them she is going to kick things off with is a whole other story.

"What do you think of this?" Gracie nervously asks Lily as she flips the camera on her iPhone to face the full-length mirror hanging on her door. "I was thinking everyone is going to expect a lot of pink and more classic punk styles from me. And I have a lot of that throughout the week. But this outfit seems like a chance to show people something that's maybe a bit more unexpected. You know, with the dress?"

Gracie stares at her reflection in the mirror. She is really proud of this look. It all started with a flowy white maxi dress she found at a thrift store with her mimi last summer. On its own, the dress was not at all her style—if anything, it more closely matched Maya's Kacey Musgraves–inspired country vibe. But Gracie had a vision. She knew there had to be a way to give it the punk twist she wanted, and she headed straight to Zoey's Closet to make it happen.

The first thing she did was cut off the dainty white spaghetti straps on the dress. In their place, she sewed on cut-up pieces of a red-and-black plaid tie she had left over from when she dressed as Avril Lavigne for Halloween one year. The cut-up tie pieces served as chunky punk-looking straps that gave the dress the edge she was craving, but Gracie knew she had to do more with it if the look was going to be worthy of the *Ardmore Aardvark Gazette*. So, over the weekend, she spent hours thrifting and came out with three black vegan leather belts: one giant one with silver studs, and two narrower ones with fun buckles. One of the buckles featured a silver skull and the other had a silver star. Gracie liked the juxtaposition

of the two. Finally, to tie it all together, Gracie threw on her favorite pair of black combat boots.

"*Gracie,*" Lily slowly says, her once sleepy eyes now wide awake. "The look is perfect. You might wind up being the best dressed person of all the best dressed people in *Ardmore Aardvark Gazette* history!"

"You sure?" Gracie asks nervously. "You don't think the maxi dress is too not-me? I thought at first about maybe ending the week with this, just to close things out with something a little different. But then I thought, why not start with it, then ease into my more usual looks?"

"I think you should definitely start with it," Lily says with a reassuring smile. "And, to be honest, I don't think the dress is not-you at all. It's a little more white and flowy than your usual, but you gave it, like, the most punk flair ever."

"Thanks, Lil," Gracie says. "Okay, I should go down and have breakfast. I have to get to school early for my photoshoot with Poppy!"

"So exciting!" Lily squeals. "Call me after school with updates!"

"Definitely," Gracie promises before hanging up.

When she gets to school at seven thirty on the dot, Poppy Martin, the school newspaper's photographer, is already waiting outside the gym with her fancy-looking Nikon camera hung around her neck.

"Gracie!" she calls as Gracie makes her way toward her. "Hey!"

"Hi, Poppy," Gracie says, an unexpected bout of shyness striking her as she realizes she's never really spoken to Poppy before. "Thanks so much for doing this."

"Are you kidding?" Poppy says. "Thank *you*. We are so lucky to have you as our feature this month. Ali showed me the old pictures of your grandma. So cool."

"Thanks!" Gracie says. "She was awesome. I can't believe I get to follow her footsteps with this."

"I can," Poppy quickly replies. "Look at your outfit! Fashion is clearly in your DNA. Everyone knows you're one of the coolest dressers in our class."

"Really?" Gracie asks, genuinely shocked. "I thought everyone just sort of knew me as the girl with pink hair and two moms."

"You have two moms?" Poppy asks. "I had no idea!"

Oh, no, Gracie thinks. *Here we go.* Gracie tries her best to be patient with people's questions about what it's like to have two moms. She knows, for the most part, people are just trying to understand her better. But sometimes it gets exhausting trying to find a way to explain something that's such a natural part of her life.

"Yep. Two moms. It's pretty much the same as having a mom and dad . . . I think," she replies, before adding with a forced laugh, "I wouldn't really know what that's like." She's given variations of the same explanation so many times at this point, it practically feels rehearsed.

"Me neither," Poppy casually replies. "I have two moms also. I always thought I was the only one in our school."

"Same!" Gracie exclaims, a little taken aback by how good it feels to meet someone who comes from a similar family background. "I heard Juni Sanchez has two dads, but other than that I thought I was the only one with same-sex parents at Ardmore Middle."

"Did you think I was going to ask what it's *really* like to have two moms?" Poppy says with a laugh. "I get that all the time."

"You do?" Gracie can't believe she finally found someone who gets where she's coming from. "I know they mean well, but it does get kind of old."

"Agreed," Poppy says. "Like, how are we even supposed to answer that? It's all we know!"

"Right!" Gracie says, nodding enthusiastically. "Whoa, it feels *really* good being able to talk about this stuff with someone who gets it."

"Yeah," Poppy says with a smile. "It does. I'm kind of bummed we never had any classes together. Imagine how much easier school could have been if we had each other all along!"

"I know," Gracie says. "Seriously."

Gracie wonders how many other people like Poppy there are in her class. Not necessarily people with two moms, but just people she might be able to connect with if she only had a chance to get to know them a little better. *Maybe I wrote my classmates off too soon,* Gracie thinks.

"So, I looked at your grandma's Best Dressed feature and it looks like all her pictures were taken by the bleachers in the gym. I thought it would be cool to take yours there too. You know, to have an obvious direct comparison. What do you think?"

"Great idea," Gracie says, resisting the urge to grab her phone right then and there to text her mama all about this. *I should save it and surprise her when the article comes out,* Gracie decides. *She's going to love this so much.*

Gracie does her best to emulate her Grandma Zoey's cool, calm vibe as she leans against the bleachers and looks into the distance while Poppy snaps a few quick shots.

"Okay," Poppy announces as she allows the camera to return to dangling around her neck. "I think we've got the shot!"

"Awesome," Gracie says. "So . . . that's it?"

"Yep!" Poppy says. "I think Ali already mentioned that you'll have a quick interview with Sue Ellen at lunch about your outfit, then you and I will meet here again tomorrow morning to capture your Day Two look."

"Perfect," Gracie says, thrilled she still has four more days of this. "Can't wait!"

The school day passes quickly. Gracie doesn't have fourth-period music with Ali, but by the time the bell rings and she puts her tone chime away, she sees he's waiting outside the door for her.

"Hey," he says as she makes her way over to him. "I was just across the hall in art class and knew you had music. Since you're sitting with the newspaper crew at lunch today for your big interview with Sue Ellen, want to walk together?"

"Sure," Gracie says, still in slight disbelief that her longtime crush knows her class schedule by heart. "I'm kind of nervous about the interview. Sue Ellen is so cool. What if she doesn't like me?"

"What are you talking about?" Ali says with a laugh. "*You* are the cool one here. You're Ardmore Middle School's best dressed! And Sue Ellen would have never let that happen if she didn't think you deserved it."

"I guess that's true," Gracie says with a nod. "It's only one question, right?"

"Yep." Ali nods. "The same question your grandma answered every day for her feature: what inspired you to pick this outfit today? Then, on Friday, she'll probably ask you a few more summarizing questions. But you two will be besties by then. I'm sure of it."

"I hope so," Gracie says, her chest constricting as they make their way over to the table by the cafeteria checkout line where the newspaper kids usually sit.

"Gracie!" Sue Ellen calls out, waving her over to the empty seat next to hers. "Come sit!"

Gracie's heart soars. The fact that Sue Ellen LePage knows her name is already cool enough in and of itself. But now she's calling her over in the middle of the cafeteria?! Gracie can feel all her classmates' eyes glued to her as she makes her way over.

"Wait," Sue Ellen instructs Gracie as she gets closer. "Before you sit down, I need a moment to take in the outfit."

"Oh," Gracie says, her face burning so hot she worries she might have instantaneously contracted some sort of fever. "It's different from my usual look, but I thought it would be a good way to switch it up. My friend Lily—well, she's more than just any old friend. I guess, the more I think about it, she's technically my best friend . . ."

The realization is a pleasant surprise for Gracie. She's never had a *best* friend before. But it's true—Lily is the one friend she knows she can count on no matter what. Her best friend.

"The dress is *perfect*," Sue Ellen interrupts Gracie's musing. "I am so hyped to feature you!"

"Wow," Gracie says, her nerves subsiding at how nice Sue Ellen is. "Thank you so much. Being featured for this column is, like, the coolest thing to have ever happened to me. I am *so* excited."

"Well, *we* are so excited to have you on board," Sue Ellen says. "And honestly? I'm hoping we can be friends. I've always thought your style was so cool. And Ali tells me you're in a fashion class?"

"Yeah," Gracie confirms, the mere thought of being in class with her P4F friends easing any lingering nerves she may have still had about talking to the most popular girl in school. "My friends and I are actually starting a business together."

"A business?" Sue Ellen looks impressed. "Girl, I'm pretty sure this feature in the *Ardmore Aardvark* is definitely not the coolest thing to have ever happened to you."

"Yeah," Gracie can't help but agree. "I guess starting a business in seventh grade *is* pretty cool."

"Okay, you ready for the interview?" Sue Ellen asks. "Maybe we could add a plug for your business in the finished piece!"

"Whoa, that would be amazing!" Gracie exclaims. "Sure, let's dive in."

After Gracie finishes explaining how she chose her outfit, she spends the rest of lunch seamlessly hitting it off with Sue Ellen, Poppy, Ali, and the rest of the newspaper kids as they tell her about their upcoming articles and she tells them all about the P4F business. *Maybe I was never really that big of an outcast at school after all*, she realizes.

"Hey," Sue Ellen calls after her as they make their way to their fifth-period classes after lunch. "If the business ever slows down, there's a spot for you on the *Ardmore Aardvark Gazette* staff. We're always looking for new fashion writers."

"Thanks, Sue Ellen," Gracie says. "The business is my main focus right now, but maybe once we get everything figured out, we could talk about it more seriously?"

"Definitely," Sue Ellen confirms. "Anyway, I've gotta jet to bio. I'll see you tomorrow at lunch!"

"See ya!" Gracie calls after her, her head held a little higher than usual as she makes her way to computer class.

seven

On Thursday, Gracie enters Zoey's Closet with a plan and goes straight to her mama.

"Mama," she begins, grabbing her sketchbook from her pink-and-black checkered tote bag she brought to school today and walking over to the workshop table. "I know you had mentioned doing a unit on crocheting today for Passion for Fashion, but I really think our focus should be on the business."

"What do you have in mind, Gracie Girl?" her mama asks. "I'm always open to suggestions."

"Well, yesterday when I was walking home from school with Sue Ellen—remember the girl from the newspaper?"

"Of course I remember," her mama says with a smile. "I'm glad you're making more friends at school."

"Same," Gracie agrees. "Especially with the P4F girls being so busy lately. It's been nice having other people to hang out with, you know?"

"You can never have too many friends," her mama says.

"Now, tell me more about what happened when you and Sue Ellen were walking."

"Oh! Yes," Gracie says. "We were walking home when we noticed that Mrs. Shlapinski down the block from school was just giving a bunch of awesome old clothes away."

"Is *that* why your mimi found five jean jackets from 1985 just lying in your closet this morning?" her mama says with a laugh. "We were wondering if you found some sort of time machine!"

"No time machine," Gracie says with a giggle. "But basically just found treasure. Mrs. Shlapinski is moving to Florida soon. She used to collect denim in the '80s and didn't feel like moving it all with her. So, I took the whole box! I was thinking maybe today the girls and I could personalize the jackets."

"What sort of personalization?" her mama asks. "Sewing? Bedazzling? Some fun patches?"

"I was sort of thinking a mix of everything. I sketched out some ideas for each of us. Look, this one's for me," Gracie says, opening her sketchbook to the page she bookmarked with a Green Day concert ticket. "It would *obviously* be punk with some metal spikes studded to the collar, and maybe some black pleather patchwork?"

"Great idea." Her mama nods, her finger gently tracing Gracie's sketch. "I definitely think we have what you need to make this happen lying around here somewhere."

"Awesome!" Gracie squeals, quickly flipping through the next few pages. "Then I have ideas for Ava, Lily, Sophia, and Maya sketched out here. Maybe some paisley patches for Maya. Some delicately embroidered flowers for Ava. Sophia could try sporty stripes going down her sleeves, and Lily could crop hers and bleach it white to give it a more crisp, cool feel."

"I think these are all wonderful," her mama says, flipping through Gracie's sketches. "But have the girls approved this? You don't want to take away a chance for them to come up with their own ideas."

Gracie sighs. "You're probably right," she groans. "But what else am I supposed to do? They're always busy! And if we spend all of class just coming up with ideas for what to do with the jackets, we'll never actually get to *making* the jackets!"

"Honey," her mama says, with one eyebrow raised. "You seem stressed. Remember what your mimi and I told you? We are all for this business as long as you are still having fun! There will be plenty of time to stress about work when you become an adult, I promise."

"Maybe I'm a *teensy* bit stressed, but that will all be over after class today," Gracie says. "This is our first time getting together as a complete group since we agreed to start the business. Hopefully they will like the jean jacket idea and we can finally start working as a team."

"Okay, the girls should be here any minute," her mama says, looking down at her watch. "Why don't you get ready to present them with your idea, and if they want to do something else, we can save crocheting as a backup?"

"Mama, there can't be a backup!" Gracie exclaims. "We have to make this work. It's our only time all week to work on the business!"

"All right, honey," her mama says, quickly rubbing her back before heading to the closet to pull out supplies. "Just try to relax, okay? Remember: *fun*."

When the girls arrive a few minutes later, Gracie is thrilled they are on time. Things are already off to a great start.

"Gracie, how is your week as best dressed going?" Lily asks as she settles into her seat. "Your outfit today is awesome."

"I agree!" Maya exclaims as she stuffs her red paisley tote bag into one of the cubbies. "Did you swap out the laces on your combat boots?"

"Yeah," Gracie says, looking down at the pink ribbon she wove in as substitute laces on her go-to black combat boots. "I found the ribbon lying around here at Zoey's Closet and I wore the boots on Monday too, so I thought this would be a fun way to spice them up."

"And is that the dress you made for the fashion show?" Sophia asks. "It still looks *so* good."

"Yes!" Gracie does a twirl so the girls can see her pink dress with black lace trim. "Sue Ellen, my new friend who's writing the piece, said that she would plug our business if I want. I thought the best way to do that would be to wear a design from the fashion show!"

"So smart." Ava nods. "Oh, sorry, I mean so *intellectual*. Our business will definitely *prosper* with ideas like that."

"So, girls, speaking of your business," Gracie's mama cuts in. "Gracie had an idea for something you could work on. I'm going to give her the floor here, but if you need me I'll be in the back doing some inventory."

"Yeah, so, about the business," Gracie says, nervously clutching her sketchbook. "I was thinking maybe we could make jean jackets for it today?"

"Weren't we supposed to crochet today?" Ava says, checking her planner. "Yep. I have it here in my planner. 'Crochet day with Ms. Anna.'"

"Yeah, we *were*," Gracie confirms. "But since this is the first time all of us have been together in a really long time, I was thinking we could actually make some jean jackets!"

Gracie rushes over to her tote bag and pulls out the five jean jackets she was just barely able to stuff in there this morning.

"I found these for us yesterday," Gracie says, passing them around the table. "I thought it would be really cool if we could each give them our own flair! I sketched out a bunch of ideas for each of us . . ."

"Wait," Ava cuts in. "You already made our designs for us?"

"Nothing is fully assigned or anything," Gracie says, pulling up her sketchbook. "I just had some ideas to move us along a little faster. Like, Ava, I thought maybe some little daisies embroidered onto the jacket could be cute."

"Doesn't making something you assigned us sort of take the passion out of Passion for Fashion?" Sophia says, flipping through Gracie's designs. "We're all here because we like being creative and coming up with designs. Isn't that the whole point of starting the business? So that we can keep being creative and coming up with designs?"

"Gracie, I'm sure your designs are great," Maya says. "But Sophia has a point. We all really like designing. This might take some of the fun out of it, you know?"

"Gracie showed me the idea she had for mine last night on FaceTime," Lily tries interjecting, her kind smile easing some of Gracie's mounting stress. "A cropped jean jacket bleached white. I'm going to use it as a jumping-off point and add lavender buttons."

"So, Lily got to see her design before the rest of us did?" Sophia frowns. "That doesn't seem fair."

"We were just FaceTiming and it came up!" Gracie blurts out. "If you girls had time to FaceTime, I would have shown you your designs too! Actually, if you had any time in general, I wouldn't have had to even make the designs in the first place because we would have spent the past couple weeks actually getting ahead on our business! Right now the only products we have are four finger knitted scarves from last week—not even a complete collection because Ava wasn't here."

The girls sit in quiet for a few seconds, looking at each other in surprise.

"Gracie is right," Ava says. "We *have* been bad about prioritizing the business lately. With all of our busy schedules, devoting P4F time to the business is the most efficient way to get things done. Let's just make the jackets. But can we at least do our own designs?"

"Sure," Gracie says with a shrug, appreciative that Ava has her back on this one. "I guess we can spend this week making our designs and getting started, then during next week's class maybe we can finish the jackets and start designing a logo for our brand."

"Oh, um, actually," Maya nervously cuts in, "I'm so sorry, Gracie, but I'm going to have to miss P4F next week. I have a choir recital at the church."

"Shoot, that reminds me, I have a dance performance that day," Sophia adds. "So I will be out then also."

"And I already told you this on FaceTime last night, but I have a soccer game that Thursday," Lily gently reminds her. "I'm sorry."

"I already sent Ms. Anna a copy of my schedule with predetermined absences ahead of the school year, but I have my first mock pre-high school entrance test next Thursday at the same time P4F is scheduled," Ava says. "It is a *gigantic* deal. I can't miss it."

"So, *none* of you will be here next week?" Gracie feels her blood starting to boil as she holds back tears. "Am I the only one who even cares about this business? When are we ever going to work on it?"

Sophia snaps back, eyeing Gracie and Lily as she says, "Well, we could've worked on it this weekend if you two weren't going to be on your exclusive trip in the Poconos."

Gracie's mouth drops open. "Are you kidding me, Sophia? All you ever do is talk about how great New York is and how much you love your weekends there," she blurts out, now yelling. "Like you ever would have ditched your precious weekends in the city for a cabin on the lake!"

She sees the hurt make its way across her friend's face and immediately knows it was the wrong thing to say.

"Sophia, I didn't even mean that . . ." Gracie begins to apologize. She knows how much Sophia has been struggling to balance her time with her dad in New York with her life with her mom and her friends here in Philly. The words just sort of flew out of Gracie's mouth before she could think better of them.

"Both of your parents live here in the same house," Sophia shoots back before Gracie can finish her apology. "You don't know what it's like to get only two days a week to see one of your parents!" She stands up. "That's it. I'm out."

Sophia grabs her things, and it's not long before Ava and Maya wordlessly shuffle out after her. Only Lily and Gracie are left at the table.

"I really messed up, didn't I?" Gracie asks Lily, a feeling of total defeat washing over her.

"To be fair, Sophia's comment about the Poconos was a little snarky," Lily says. "But, um, yes. You were probably a bit out of line there."

Gracie gulps hard. Yes, she wants the business to work more than anything. But does she even like the side of herself that working on it is bringing out?

eight

"There's our best dressed girl!" Gracie's mimi cheers as Gracie makes her way down the stairs into the kitchen. "Is this the final look of the week?"

"Yep." Gracie nods. "The weather is warmer than I expected, so I had to change it at the last minute."

For her final look, Gracie originally planned to wear a chunky, neon pink sweater dress paired with knee-high black combat boots that she adorned with spiky silver studs going up the sides. The look was pretty awesome. But rather than being a brisk fifty-degree day like the weather app on her iPhone promised it would be when she was planning her outfits last Sunday, the weather is shockingly warm today—eighty-two degrees, to be exact. When Gracie opened her window in the morning, she felt a gust of the warm air and knew she had to pivot. Instead, she opted for a pair of baggy black camo pants and a neon pink polo with tiny studs on the collar that she made with her mama years ago.

"The look is simpler than what I was going for originally," Gracie tells her mimi. "But I feel like it achieves a similar vibe."

"I think you look *fantastic*," her mimi says, a wide smile making its way across her face. "And I made your favorite breakfast in honor of the last day! Vanilla bean waffles with a side of fresh blueberries from the farmer's market."

Gracie inhales deeply. The smell of vanilla is so pungent and delicious that she wishes she could bottle it up and use it as a perfume. Usually, she would be diving headfirst into a short stack of her mimi's delicious waffles. But she doesn't have much of an appetite this morning.

"I actually think I might skip breakfast this morning, Mimi," Gracie says, trying to sound casual. "I have my last photoshoot with Poppy today. I should get there extra early."

"It's six forty-five, and it takes ten minutes to walk from here to school," her mimi says, nodding toward the clock on the oven. "I know you have to get to school early, but don't you think a whole hour early might be a bit excessive? Max won't even be up for another hour, and his school starts the same time as yours."

"I don't know," Gracie says with a shrug, still trying desperately to avoid talking about the real reason she wants to leave early. "Poppy might need some extra pictures."

"Then all the more reason to eat up," her mimi says, pushing the plate toward her. "You'll need the extra stamina for your big photoshoot."

"I . . . I'm just not that hungry," Gracie says, pushing the plate back. "Sorry."

"Don't be sorry, sweetie," her mimi says, grabbing Gracie's plate and setting it aside on the counter. "You don't have to eat if you don't feel like it. I told you about the one time your Grandpa Ned forced me to eat cherry pie when I was your age and I vomited. Ugh. Terrible. I will *never* do that to my child."

"Thanks, Mimi," Gracie says with a small grin before getting out of her seat. "I guess I should get going to school then."

"Not so fast, missy," her mimi says, gesturing for Gracie to sit back down. "You don't need to eat breakfast, but it is definitely way too early to head to school. And you know I love my quality morning time with you! Tell me what's going on. Are you nervous for your last day of the fashion feature?"

"Actually no," Gracie answers honestly. "If anything, I'm pretty excited. I've had so much fun hanging out with the newspaper kids, I can't wait to spend another day hanging with them at school."

"You know you can be friends with them after this week too, right?" her mimi says. "You don't need to be Ardmore's best dressed to deserve a seat at that table."

"Yeah." Gracie nods. "I was kind of nervous about that, but Sue Ellen told me yesterday that I should sit with them at lunch even after the feature is done. And Poppy even offered to show me how to do photography. She said I could have a good eye for street style—or 'hall style,' in this case. They basically just have someone go around taking pictures of the best dressed people in the school hallways."

"That sounds *so* fun," her mimi says with a smile. "Are you going to do it?"

"I don't know," Gracie says with a sigh. "It's just . . ."

"What is it, Gracie Girl?" her mimi asks. "Something has obviously got you down. Is it what happened with your friends at Zoey's Closet yesterday? Your mama filled me in a bit before bed last night."

Gracie feels her eyes welling up at the mention of the fight. This is *exactly* why she didn't want to talk about it this morning. She knew that as soon as she did, it would make her all emotional. Then how will her pictures going to turn out? She can't be best dressed with red, teary eyes!

"I really shouldn't be thinking about this right now," Gracie says, quickly wiping her eyes with the tie-dyed linen napkin on the table. "My eyes will look all sad and puffy in the newspaper pictures."

"Hey, you know the best way to get over the sadness?" her mimi says gently. "It's to *accept* the sadness. Once you accept it, we can work on overcoming the pain that comes along with it. Come on, spill the beans. Get it all out. We'll splash your face with some ice water once you've gotten it all off your chest. I promise that will take care of the puffy eyes."

"Okay, fine," Gracie says, sniffling into the napkin. "It's just . . . I was so excited about this business, you know? And I tried to be really patient. I know I'm not always good at that, like when we have long car rides and stuff, but I promise I was actually being patient with this! I didn't even bring it up the second time. I purposely waited until someone else did so that I could be sure I wasn't just rushing them into my idea."

"That *is* very patient of you," her mimi says with an understanding nod before jokingly adding, "I hope we can channel some of that patience when we drive to the cabin this afternoon."

"I will, I promise," Gracie says with a small giggle. "But anyway, I really, really was trying so hard. Then it finally seemed like everyone was on board with it that night at Maya's, so I got excited! And I started planning! But it just has not seemed like anyone is as excited or into planning as I am. Except for Lily. But even she's pretty busy with soccer and her bat mitzvah coming up."

"Have you tried telling your friends how you feel?" her mimi asks. "The root to so many issues is usually just a little miscommunication."

"Yeah, well, I tried to tell them last night, but things got *super* out of hand," Gracie says, shuddering at the memory. "I sort of blew up, then Sophia called me out for only inviting Lily to the Poconos, then I *really* exploded and made a comment that sort of implied she likes hanging out in New York more than she likes being here with us."

"Yikes," her mimi says. "It sounds like things really escalated there. Have you tried apologizing?"

"I tried texting her," Gracie says. "But she didn't reply. And honestly? I'm still pretty hurt that everyone isn't taking P4F or the business as seriously as I am."

"Well, if there's anything I've learned from all of the many episodes of *Shark Tank* I've watched with your brother, it's that you can't take business personally," her mimi says. "Your friends may be too busy to work on the business, but they aren't too busy for *you*. Don't forget the difference there."

"Yeah, but sometimes it feels like it's both," Gracie admits, a fresh stream of tears making its way down her face. "I just miss hanging out all the time like we did in the summer, and starting a business seemed like a great way to do that."

"Sounds like everyone is just finding the right path for them right now," her mimi says. "It's a new school year, you all are meeting new friends, and you don't even go to the same schools. This is healthy!"

"Then why do I feel so sad?" Gracie asks through sniffles. "Shouldn't it feel good if it's healthy?"

"Oh, honey," her mimi says, wrapping her arms around Gracie for a hug. "Just focus on all the great things you have coming up. A full day of hanging with your newspaper friends, chatting about your outfit. Then we head off to the Poconos with Lily!"

"That's true," Gracie concedes. "I do have a fun day ahead."

"How's this for a plan?" her mimi begins. "We splash your face with cold water, you dominate your last day as best dressed, and you spend the rest of the weekend decompressing from all this stress you've put on yourself with this business. Then, once we're back, you can think about how to handle the business and things with your friends with a fresh, clear mind."

Gracie takes a deep breath. "That sounds good," she says, giving her mimi a hug. She feels her shoulders slightly untense. "You're right. Talking it through does kind of make me feel better."

Thinking about what happened last night and the radio silence she's gotten from Sophia, Ava, and Maya since then still makes Gracie feel uneasy. But knowing she has a Mimi-approved plan for the day makes it feel just a bit more manageable. Gracie's mimi always gives the right advice.

nine

"Okay, last question," Sue Ellen says as they wrap up their final interview for the week. "What is it that draws you to fashion?"

"Hmm . . ." Gracie considers the question carefully before answering. "I think I just like how creative it is. I grew up in a super creative house—my mimi is a painter and my mama owns Zoey's Closet a few streets over from school. So, I've grown up trying all sorts of artsy things—finger painting, paper mache, ceramics, all of it. But something about fashion is extra exciting for me. I like how I can actually *wear* the creativity on my body. Like, people can look at me and instantly know what I'm all about just by what I threw together. Does that make sense?"

"Totally." Sue Ellen nods, putting her phone away after stopping the recorder app. "And that's a wrap! Gracie, you crushed it."

"Seriously," Poppy chimes in. "You want to see some of the edited pictures from earlier this week?"

"Sure," Gracie says, walking to the other side of the lunch table to see the photos Poppy has open on her computer screen. The pictures are awesome. She had Gracie pose exactly where her Grandma Zoey did, and Poppy even edited the shots to give them that same '70s vintage vibe that the photos of Grandma Zoey had.

"Whoa," Gracie musters, her mouth agape. "Poppy, these are *so* good!"

"Thanks," Poppy says, a proud smile breaking across her face. "I've been working extra hard to get the exact filter right to match your Grandma Zoey's, but I think I finally nailed it."

"You definitely did," Gracie agrees, settling back into her seat next to Sue Ellen's. "I can't wait to see the full piece!"

"I think this is going to be one of the most iconic Best Dressed features we've done in a long time," Sue Ellen says.

"Thanks," Gracie says, blushing. "And, um, this has been really fun for me. It might be the best week I've had at school, like, ever."

"You're still going to hang out with us after this week, right?" Ali asks from the other side of the table. "And *maybe* even consider joining newspaper?"

"Definitely to the hanging out, and maybe to the newspaper," Gracie responds, a little more open to the idea of joining the newspaper than she has been before. Why should she be the only P4F girl holding out on other extracurriculars? If nobody else is prioritizing the business, maybe it's her time to put it on the back burner too.

School passes by quickly, and before she knows it, Gracie is in the packed car with her family and Lily, ready to hit the road. By the time they make it to the Poconos, Gracie is feeling like a completely different person from the girl who was crying at the breakfast table this morning. The great day at school with her new friends was already enough to lift her spirits, but being back at her family's cabin here fully catapults her spirits straight up to the cotton candy-pink sky. She doesn't realize how much she missed this place until they are sitting on the patio, roasting marshmallows as they watch the sun set over the lake. Just the smell of their makeshift bonfire wafting around the crisp, woodsy air melts away any last worry she was clinging on to.

Gracie stares out at the deep blue lake, images of the sprawling mountains and fall leaves reflecting onto the calm water.

"You know," Gracie tells her family and Lily as her marshmallow crisps in the bonfire, "I was pretty bummed that the weather warmed up because it meant I had to switch my outfit for today, but it wound up being the best thing."

"A little surprise sunshine is never a bad thing," her mama says. "Especially when it turns into a warm night like this."

"Is it usually super cold here at night?" Lily asks. "I love that we can just be in T-shirts."

"Cold?" Max says. "Try *freezing*. I never want to do nighttime bonfires."

"This time of the year it isn't so bad," Gracie's mimi says. "But we definitely are not normally sitting here in T-shirts and shorts. It's usually more big sweatshirts and cozy blankets."

"That sounds kind of nice in its own way too," Lily says. "My mom and I used to love bundling up on cold nights for bonfires outside when we'd go to the Catskills. We even finger knitted a giant blanket just for our cold Catskills nights."

"I remember you mentioned you and your mom loved finger knitting together," Gracie's mama says. "On the first day of Passion for Fashion class, right?"

"Yeah." Lily nods. "I was so excited that we were going to be doing it. Half of missing her is missing all of the stuff we used to do together, you know? I love my dad, but he's not exactly great at crafting."

"Well, honey, if you ever are feeling the itch to craft, you've got two moms who live for crafting right here," Gracie's mimi says, reaching over to give Lily a warm hug. "We are always here for that."

"I am too!" Max sweetly chimes in. "I'm a pretty good crafter. Well, except for that one time I knit my own socks and wound up with a giant hole where my toes were supposed to go."

Gracie laughs. "Yeah, I remember that. Knitting might just not be your thing, Max."

"Your brother is *not* a bad knitter, Gracie," her mama says. "What he made was excellent. They just weren't socks. More *leg warmers.*"

Max nods. "Mama has a point. They were great leg warmers. I wore them for '80s day at school and my legs were *so* warm."

Everyone giggles.

"So, Gracie, Lily, how are you girls feeling about everything after Thursday?" Gracie's mama asks. "Have you talked to the other girls at all? I'm sorry I wasn't there when that all happened. I should have rushed out to mediate."

"I haven't texted them today," Lily says. "I meant to, but the day just got away from me. School was so busy, then I had my cantor's class, then we were heading here."

Gracie lets out a sharp exhale. Just the thought of the drama tenses her right up.

"I was sort of hoping I could take a break from thinking about that this weekend," Gracie says, her eyes meeting her mimi's as she reaffirms their plan. "And the business too. Maybe we can just unwind a bit while we're here."

"That sounds great to me," Lily says, carefully placing her toasted marshmallow over the singular Hershey's chocolate square she has lined up on her graham cracker. "My phone doesn't have service here anyway, so I'm not sure what we could even do."

"Mine either," Gracie says. "I just turned it off and left it in our room. Might as well embrace the off-the-grid life."

"I have a feeling this is going to be *just* what the doctor ordered for you girls," her mimi says, taking a large bite out of her s'more. "Some time to relax, have fun, and focus on just being kids."

The next day they all wake up bright and early to go on a sunrise hike. By the time they reach the peak, the sky is so pink it almost perfectly mirrors the color of Gracie's hair.

"Lily! We should take a selfie!" Gracie exclaims before remembering with a laugh that they both had left their phones in the cabin.

"Here," her mama says, pulling her disposable camera out of her backpack. "Let me take one of you girls the old-fashioned way."

Gracie squeezes her pal tightly as her mom snaps a few pictures of them standing on the edge of the beautiful cliff overlooking the lake and the mountains.

"I wish we could see how they turned out," Gracie laments. "What if we're just two shadows in front of the sun?"

"Then you're just two shadows in the sun!" her mama says. "That's the fun of using a disposable camera. No use in fussing over how the picture turned out. You just take it, hope for the best, and move forward."

"Plus, there's all of that anticipation!" Gracie's mimi adds. "When you take a picture on an iPhone, you take it, dwell on it for twenty minutes, maybe post it online, then never think about it again. But with disposables, you have something to look forward to. Once we're back home when this trip is over, you'll get to go to the store, get these pictures developed, and then relive this very moment staring at this beautiful sunrise on the cliff."

"That is kind of cool," Lily admits. "I always like having things to look forward to."

"Me too," Gracie's mimi says with a smile. "That's what keeps life interesting, right?"

"I guess it is kind of nice to take a picture and not instantly worry about whether or not I'm gonna post it," Gracie admits. "Maybe this relaxing stuff is for me after all."

After their hike, they head back down to the cabin to help Gracie's mimi bake a wide array of pies for their family tradition at the cabin—pie night. They make five savory pies and five sweet ones, and then they do a taste test to decide which pies deserve to be in the top three. Fridays are, of course, usually Shabbat night with the P4F girls, but since they can't be with the rest of the girls, they decide to skip it this week.

"Ms. Brie, I think this pie is ready to go," Lily says to Gracie's mimi as she brushes the egg wash over the crust of the cheeseburger pie she was working on. "What do I do now?"

"Oh, that looks *gorgeous*, Lily," Gracie's mimi says, grabbing Lily's pie and gently placing it into the oven. "Now all that's left to do is dance."

"Dance?" Lily asks, confused. "What do you mean?"

"In our family, the tradition is to do a victory dance whenever someone completes their pie," Gracie's mimi explains. "You pick the song and we all dance around the kitchen!"

"You don't have to do it," Gracie says, worried her shy friend might be nervous. "It's just a silly tradition."

"No!" Lily insists. "That sounds like the most fun tradition. Do you have 'Boogie Shoes' somewhere? My mom and I used to love dancing around to that while she made Shabbat dinner."

"Mama has that on vinyl!" Max exclaims, rushing over to the record collection in the living area. "Can someone help me play this?"

"You got it, hon," his mama says with a laugh, throwing the record on. Before they know it, "Boogie Shoes" is blasting through the little cabin and they're all dancing around the kitchen.

Gracie looks over at Lily doing the limbo under a makeshift bridge her moms created by tying a few old dish rags together and notices her friend seems happier and more carefree than she's seen her since she got here.

"Hey, Gracie," Lily says before they go to bed later that night, their bellies filled with pie. "Thanks for inviting me this weekend."

"Of course," Gracie says. "Inviting you was a no-brainer! I'm so glad you came. You have to start coming with us every time, okay?"

"Definitely," Lily agrees. "I just . . . I didn't realize how much I missed being with a complete family. I mean, my dad and I have each other . . . but it can be hard needing everything from one person all the time if that's not how we used to be when my mom was here. It's nice being around two parents, you know?"

"Yeah, well, you can be around my moms whenever you want," Gracie says. "It's so fun having you around."

And she means it. Before meeting Lily, Gracie would roll her eyes at the girls at school with their matching Best Friend bracelets and BFF appreciation posts on social media. But now, thanks to Lily, she finally gets the hype.

ten

The rest of the weekend is spent kayaking on the lake, going on long bike rides, cooking up delicious meals with their finds at the local farmer's market, and exchanging spooky stories around the bonfire. As far as Gracie is concerned, it has been pure bliss. "I don't want this weekend to be over," Gracie laments as she scarfs down the last of the leftover apple pie she's having for breakfast. "It was the best."

"I know," Lily agrees. "Who knew you could have this much fun without Wi-Fi?"

"I did," Gracie's moms say in unison before the whole table bursts into laughter.

"This was a super fun weekend and all," Max says, "but I'm ready to get back to video games."

"Remember, mister, only half an hour of video games a day," his mama says. "We don't want that brilliant little brain of yours turning to mush now, do we?"

"Only half an hour," Max agrees. "Fine. I promise!"

"What do you all think of one last dance party before we hit the road?" his mimi suggests. "Just to shake out any nerves we may have about getting back to reality."

"Yes!" Lily agrees, softly clapping her hands together. "Please!"

"Okay, Lily, because you seem the most excited here, I think we should do 'Boogie Shoes' in your honor," Gracie's mimi says with a smile. "Unless you have another song request."

"'Boogie Shoes' is perfect!" Lily says. "Thank you."

"No, thank *you*," Gracie's mimi says. "This is one of my favorite songs and I haven't listened to it for way too long until this weekend."

She gets the song going on the record player and the whole group gets up and starts dancing around the living room, Gracie and Lily laughing hard as they take turns doing silly dances like the funky chicken and the worm.

"All right, folks," Gracie's mama says as the song comes to a close. "I hate to be the bearer of bad news, but I think we really do have to go now if we want to beat traffic."

Gracie's high spirits quickly come crashing down as soon as they get back in the car. Leaving the Poconos means getting back to reality, and Gracie remembers that she still hadn't made up with her P4F friends yet since Thursday. She just cannot imagine a reality without her new besties. Yes, Lily is quickly becoming her very best friend. But the rest of the crew is just as important to her.

She turns her phone off airplane mode once they drive into an area she knows has better service, hoping a text from Sophia might make its way through to her. Maybe even some casual chitchat in the P4F group text. But nothing. Zip. Zilch. Nada. *Maybe it's just a glitch because I haven't had service for so long,* she thinks, turning off her phone and turning it back on for good measure. But still nothing.

"Hey, do you all have service here?" Gracie asks the rest of the car, seeing full bars on her screen but hoping maybe it's wrong.

"Yep," Max confirms. "My phone is blowing up!"

"I have service too," their mama says. "I'm getting some new emails coming in now."

"Yep," Lily says. "I was just able to text my dad."

Gracie looks over at Lily's phone and notices her finger now hovering over the silent P4F group text. Her heart sinks. She had not even fully considered Lily in all of this. Lily is not the one who was allowed to invite only one friend to the Poconos. It's not her fault Gracie picked her to come! And it's definitely not her fault Gracie freaked out at Sophia the other night. But it sounds like Lily's caught in between Gracie and everyone else.

Gracie feels awful. She doesn't want to put her friend in this position. But what can she do? How does she fix this? Did she mess it up too badly to be fixed at this point? Her heart sinks even lower at the thought of losing them forever.

"I miss them," Lily quietly says to Gracie, seemingly reading her mind. "We have to fix this."

"We do," Gracie agrees. "And I'm sorry you got dragged into all this drama. I feel like it was all my fault."

"Don't worry," Lily says with a reassuring smile. "Things just got heated for everyone involved. It wasn't just you. It sort of felt like everyone's tensions were high."

"I guess that's true," Gracie says. "But how do we fix it? How can we bring the tensions back down?"

"Hmm," Lily wonders aloud. "Remember when we were planning the fashion show and there was that big fight?"

"Yeah, of course," Gracie says, thinking back to Zoey's Closet when it was flooded a few months ago and everyone was yelling at each other for different reasons. "I still feel guilty about that day."

"You shouldn't," Lily says. "Because you fixed it, remember? You suggested hanging out for the weekend at your house so we could talk everything out."

"You're right," Gracie says. "But we have to go even bigger this time. It feels like they're really upset."

"What are you thinking?" Lily asks. "Still a weekend?"

"Yeah," Gracie says slowly as she nods. "I think Sophia mentioned that she's skipping New York next weekend too because her dad is going to be in Europe for business. So maybe we invite everyone over to my house. Friday night we can have Shabbat and a slumber party where we can really sort out the drama. Once that's hopefully resolved, we can spend Saturday discussing the business and getting on the same page."

"And maybe a movie on Saturday night," Lily suggests. "Gracie, I know *Clueless* is usually our go-to with the P4F girls, but have you seen *Funny Face*? It's this classic old movie from, like, the 1950s or something. It's about a regular girl who becomes a big fashion model. My aunt and I watched it once and it's full of old-timey fashion inspo. Maybe we could all watch it together?"

"That's a great idea," Gracie says. "Perfect. Mimi! Mama! Can I have the girls over next weekend?"

Her moms lower the volume on their podcast and listen to Gracie and Lily's proposed plan.

"I'm all in for you restoring your relationship with the girls," Gracie's mama says. "There's no sense in letting some silly drama get in the way of such a tight bond."

"I agree," Gracie's mimi says. "And I'm glad you want to have everyone at our house, Gracie. How would you feel about a paint party on Saturday to get the creative juices flowing before the big business brainstorm?"

"What do you think, Lily?" Gracie asks. "Does painting sound fun?"

"Very," Lily confirms. "Let's text the girls now."

After half an hour of carefully going back and forth on exactly how to word it, Lily and Gracie come up with a message.

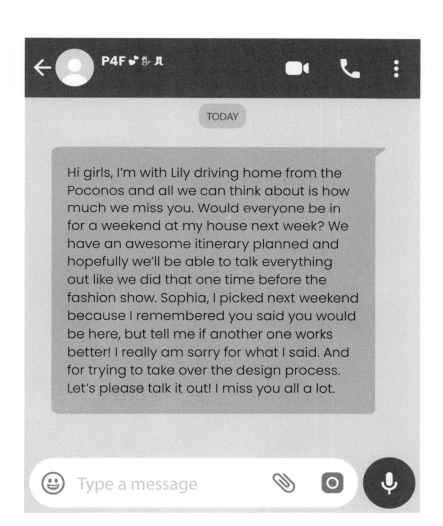

The girls stare down at their phones nervously for what feels like hours until their phones finally light up with a text from Maya.

Maya
Y'all know I don't believe in holding grudges. Sure! I'll see you next weekend. 😊

A few minutes later, Ava chimes in.

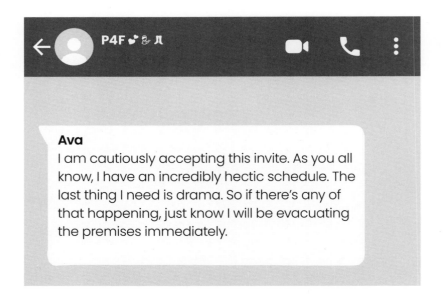

Ava
I am cautiously accepting this invite. As you all know, I have an incredibly hectic schedule. The last thing I need is drama. So if there's any of that happening, just know I will be evacuating the premises immediately.

"Okay, now we just have to wait and see if Sophia accepts," Gracie says, staring at her phone like it's Ali Mansourian the day he first showed up to school with his cute shaggy new haircut. "*If* she accepts."

"It's a good sign that Ava accepted," Lily reassures. "I don't think Ava would have accepted if she didn't already talk to Sophia about it."

"Yeah." Gracie nods. "That's a good point. Okay, fingers crossed."

The text doesn't come in until two hours later, after Gracie's moms drop Lily off at her house, pop into Trader Joe's to pick up groceries for the week, and finally pull into their own driveway. Gracie eagerly unlocks her phone to see Sophia's message.

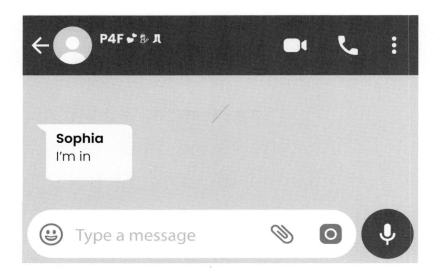

It may be just two words and not necessarily the most enthusiastic RSVP she's ever seen, but Gracie lets out a giant sigh of relief. *She's in*, which means Gracie has a real shot at cleaning up this mess. The last thing she wants is to lose the first group of friends that have fully accepted her. And she'll do everything she can to make sure that doesn't happen.

eleven

"So, are you excited for the paper with your fashion feature?" Ali asks Gracie as they walk home from school on Monday. "It should be out this Friday!"

"Wow," Gracie says, her stomach doing a small somersault. "I didn't think it would be so soon! I had a lot of fun working with Sue Ellen and Poppy, and the pictures Poppy took were *super* awesome. I just hope my answers to Sue Ellen's questions were good enough. And my outfits! Like, maybe I should have just done two belts for Monday's outfit? Was it even punk enough? I hope people don't think I'm some sort of mainstream sellout!"

"I'm not really a fashion guy," Ali says with a shrug, before adding with a shy smile, "but for what it's worth, I thought all of your outfits were *very* cool and *very* punk."

Gracie feels her cheeks burn at Ali's compliment. "Thanks, Ali," she says, hoping he'll quickly change the subject so her face can return to a normal temperature.

"Of course," he says. "How's the business coming along? I'm sure the article will be great promo for it!"

"Well, we sort of hit a snag with the business last week," Gracie admits, lifting her flowy black lace skirt as she hops over a puddle on the side of the road. "And I guess part of it was my fault."

"What do you mean? What happened?" Ali asks. "You seemed so excited about it!"

"I think I might have been a little *too* excited about it," Gracie says with a sigh. She tells Ali what happened at Zoey's Closet and then about the Poconos thing, all the while looking down at her feet to avoid his eyes. "I kind of snapped and said some things I didn't mean," she finishes.

"I know how you feel," Ali says kindly to her. "I snap sometimes too."

"Really?" Gracie asks, totally thrown off by his response. "You do? But you always seem so . . . *calm*."

"Most of the time I am," Ali says. "But sometimes I get really worked up and I wind up saying things I don't mean. Then I feel super guilty for whatever it is I said. It happens less now, but it used to happen all the time when I was younger. Hey, weren't you there for my meltdown during Field Day in fifth grade?"

Gracie thinks for a minute before she recalls the time Ali stomped off their elementary school's playground after his team lost the annual tug-of-war competition.

"Oh yeah," Gracie says. "I honestly forgot about that."

"I was so embarrassed," Ali says, sheepishly looking down. "I totally freaked out on all my teammates and the whole school saw me march off the playground crying like a baby. I didn't even want to come back to school the following Monday."

"But you did," Gracie reminds him. "And everything was fine, right?"

"Yeah, I guess so . . . I had to do some major apologizing to my teammates, who also happened to be my friends," Ali says. "But they all forgave me. And I've really tried to work on my snapping since then."

"I hope my friends can forgive me the way yours did," Gracie says, her chest tightening. "I was pretty hard on Sophia."

"Well, it happened last week, right?" Ali asks. "Have you all talked since?"

"Sort of," Gracie says. "It was radio silence for a while in the group chat, but after our time in the Poconos, Lily and I decided I should have all the girls over my house this weekend for a giant slumber party to talk everything out. I don't even care about the business anymore. I just want my friends back."

"They did seem pretty awesome when I met them at the fashion show," Ali says. "I'm sure you'll work it out."

"I hope so," Gracie says with a sigh. "I wish we could just come together the way we did for the fashion show."

"Yeah, that was so cool how you all helped your friend as a team," Ali says as they approach their street. "Whose hometown was wrecked by the hurricane again? Maya?"

"Yeah . . . wait," Gracie says, a lightbulb going off in her head. "Ali! That's it!"

"Um, what?" Ali asks, scratching his head. "What's it?"

"I'll explain later," Gracie says excitedly, running toward her house. "I have to tell my mimi!"

She is panting by the time she gets to her doorstep, but she doesn't let that stop her. "Mimi!" Gracie yells, bursting through the front door. "Are you here?"

"Hey, honey bunny!" her mimi shouts from upstairs. "I'm in the studio!"

Gracie races up the stairs into the studio to find her in a paint-covered smock, finishing up an abstract self-portrait.

"You okay, sweetie?" her mimi asks, one eyebrow raised. "You seem a little out of breath."

"I am," Gracie says, her hands on her knees as she forces herself to slowly exhale. "I just ran up the stairs. I was so excited to talk to you."

"Well, now *I* am excited to hear what you have to say!" her mimi says, setting her brush down. "What's up?"

"I was filling Ali in on everything that's been happening with the business and the P4F girls," Gracie shares quickly. "Then we were talking about the fashion show, because that's where he met them all, remember? And he was saying how it was so cool that we all united to *help* Maya."

"That was very cool," her mimi says, nodding. "So, what's the big revelation here?"

"It got me thinking," Gracie says. "My favorite part of the fashion show was that even though we had our differences along the way, the girls and I were all so eager about *helping* Maya. I loved how we came together to help our friend. So, maybe I've been thinking about this business thing all wrong. Maybe it's not a *business* that we should be starting. Maybe it's a charity that features fashion for a cause."

"Oh, what a great idea!" her mimi says, clapping her hands with excitement. "I'm sure the girls will love it."

"You think so?" Gracie asks nervously. "I wanted to check with you first. I don't exactly trust my gut with what to do when it comes to my friends right now."

"Honey, first of all, you have a *wonderful* gut and I think you should be trusting it," her mimi says with a smile. "But if you'd like my input, yes. I agree this is a great idea."

"This way we can give back while still being creative and working together, you know?" Gracie says. "And it doesn't have to be as intense as the business. We can take it more slowly and only focus our attention on causes we really care about."

"Wonderful," her mimi says. "I'm so proud of you and I cannot wait to see what your friends have to say about it this weekend!"

"Are ya kidding me?" Gracie jokingly asks with a hand on her hip. "There is no *way* I am waiting for this weekend. I have to text them right now!"

Gracie quickly pulls her phone out of the pocket of her oversized denim jacket and starts typing away.

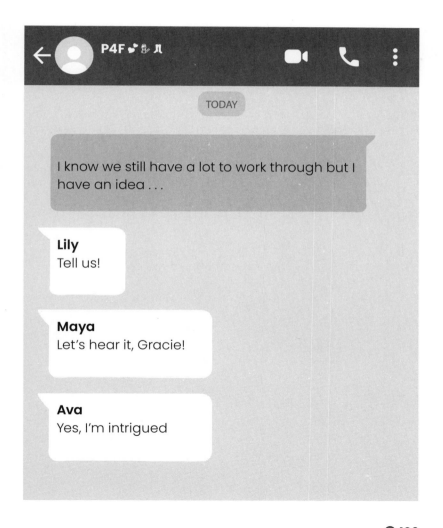

Sophia
Just had to look up "intrigued," but same

So . . . what if instead of our business we did a charity featuring fashion for a cause? Coming together to help Maya's hometown was so awesome. What if we just forgot about the business and did more stuff like that?

Maya
If there's one thing I love, it's giving back. Count me in!

Ava
I need to hear more, but I am definitely interested

Ava
**assuredly interested—shoot, forgot to use a vocab word!

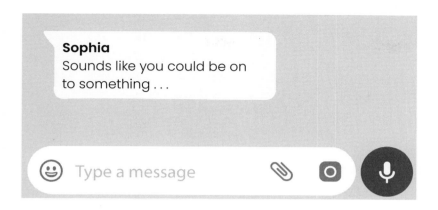

Sophia
Sounds like you could be on to something . . .

Type a message

Before Gracie can draft a response, her phone lights up with a call from Lily.

"Gracie, this is such a good idea!" Lily exclaims in her quiet way as soon as Gracie answers. "You even got a positive response from Sophia."

"I was worried she would still be too mad at me to even respond," Gracie says. "But I guess I had some hope after she agreed to the sleepover this weekend."

"I bet she's ready to forgive and move on," Lily says. "We all miss each other, and if there are two things we are passionate about, it's fashion and giving back. I think this weekend is going to snap us back to normal."

"I sure hope so," Gracie says, a nervous knot forming in her stomach. If she and her friends can't work through their differences and come together this weekend, then what happens? Gracie's heart starts beating faster at the very thought. *This weekend needs to be perfect,* she concludes. *It's the only solution.*

twelve

"**M**ama!" Gracie shouts as she comes running into Zoey's Closet Friday after school. "It's here! It's here!"

"Gracie?" her mama calls out from her office. "Is that you?"

"Who else would it be?" Gracie asks with a giggle. "Do you have a secret daughter I don't know about?"

"No secret daughter," her mama replies with a laugh. "Does your mimi know you're here? I thought the plan was to meet at home in an hour, then go shopping to prep for the big sleepover this weekend."

"It was," Gracie says. "But I told Mimi I have to come here first because I have something super special that I'm just can't wait to show you."

Gracie cautiously hands her mama her copy of the *Ardmore Aardvark Gazette*.

"The Best Dressed feature came out today," Gracie explains. "And you're the first person I wanted to show it to."

When her mama opens the paper, Gracie can't contain her grin when she sees the headline:

7TH GRADE'S BEST DRESSED
Grace Alexander-Cline

Taking up a whole page of the paper, the fashion feature begins with how fashion runs in the family for Gracie and where her style inspiration comes from. As Gracie's mama reads, she wraps her free arm around Gracie and gives her a tight squeeze.

"I grew up in a super creative house," Gracie's mama reads aloud a quote Gracie gave about where she drew her fashion inspiration. "My mimi is a painter and my mama owns Zoey's Closet a few streets over from school. So, I've grown up trying all sorts of artsy things—finger painting, paper mache, ceramics, all of it."

After the intro detailing Gracie's backstory, the article continues with photos of Gracie next to photos of her Grandma Zoey for each day of the week, followed by a quote from something Gracie said in her interviews with Sue Ellen. Thursday's outfit was Gracie's favorite, since she wore the dress she made for the charity show and Sue Ellen included a nod to Zoey's Closet and the P4F girls in the description. But the looks she chose for Tuesday and Wednesday were tied as close seconds.

At the very end of the article, Sue Ellen even managed to include a plug for Gracie and the rest of the P4F girls: *Can't get enough of Gracie and her style? Stay tuned! She and her fashionable friends have a very exciting project in the works.*

"Oh, Gracie," her mama says, tears welling up in her eyes as she takes in each of the pictures. "This is the most special thing. I have to get it framed!"

"Thanks, Mama," Gracie shyly replies. "You don't have to read all my quotes now. I know it's kind of a lot. You can read it later."

TUESDAY

GRACIE

ZOEY

"This is an outfit that I would throw on any day, feature or not. The punk band tee with pants and combat boots feels like an easy uniform for me to pull from."

"Read it later?" her mama says, proudly scanning the feature. "I can't wait until later! This is too exciting."

She opens the interview reads quietly, before setting it down on her desk and pulling Gracie in for a big hug.

"Honey, I am *so* proud of you," she says. "I wish Grandma Zoey was here to see this. She would have been over the moon."

By the time Gracie and her mama make it back to their house, Lily is already there waiting for them with Gracie's mimi. Lily and Gracie both get half days on Fridays at school, so they agreed Lily would get dropped off at Gracie's house as soon as she was out so that they could prep for the big sleepover together.

WEDNESDAY

GRACIE

ZOEY

"I spent forever collecting these patches. Some of them were my mimi's, some were my mama's, and a bunch I found at thrift stores. I sewed them onto an old pair of jeans I had never wore, and now they're my favorite pair!"

"Ms. Brie told me that the article came out!" Lily exclaims as soon as Gracie walks in. "Can I see?"

"Sure," Gracie says, a proud smile breaking across her face as she reaches for a copy of the paper from her backpack. "They gave me, like, four copies! Mama is going to get one of them framed, but I still have three in here."

"Ooh, I can't wait to see this," her mimi squeals. "Our little girl is a fashion star!"

Gracie hands her mimi and Lily each their own copy and they quietly look through them as they sit across from each other at the kitchen table.

"Oh, Gracie," her mimi says. "This is wonderful."

"Gracie, this is so special," Lily says with a smile. "All your outfits were perfect . . . Also, on that note, your outfit today is *so* cool."

"Thanks," Gracie says, looking down at the loose-fitting silky pants she paired with a chunky black sweater and black combat boots. "I feel like there's all this pressure to keep it up after this feature!"

"Just be yourself and wear what you feel most comfortable in," her mama reassures with a comforting smile. "That's all that matters."

"Yep," her mimi agrees with a nod. "You have all the right fashion instincts in that beautiful little noggin of yours. Not to mention all the fashion inspiration you must get from your fashionista friends!"

Gracie takes a look at Lily, who currently looks like the epitome of classic cool dressed in high-waisted mom jeans, a sleeveless white sweater, and pointed flat leather mules. Their styles may be different, but each of the P4F girls really knows how to dress.

"You're right," Gracie agrees, shooting her friend a smile. "I have the most fashionable friends ever."

"Well, speaking of your friends," her mama begins, "what do you girls say we start shopping for this slumber party?"

When they get to the grocery store, Gracie's moms go to the cleaning aisle to pick up some household items while Lily and Gracie focus on the food. "As far as snacks go, I think we have to do a mix of salty and sweet," Gracie says. "What do you think?"

"Great idea." Lily nods. "Ava always has a sweet tooth, but

I've noticed Maya usually craves things on the saltier side. It will be good to have both!"

"Perfect," Gracie says, grabbing some fruity gummies and some chocolates from the candy aisle where they're currently stationed. "Now, want to head to the chips section for some salty?"

"Sure," Lily says, following along as Gracie walks over to the candy aisle. "So, wait, I can't believe I didn't ask—did you get to talk to Ali about your feature?"

"Yeah," Gracie says, her face reddening at the mention of his name. "We didn't get to walk home from school today because he had newspaper, but he met me outside my front door this morning so that he could hand deliver my copies."

"Gracie, that's so cute," Lily says as they enter the chip aisle of the grocery store. "Do you still have a crush on him?"

"For sure," Gracie says with a nod, slightly embarrassed to be discussing this, even with her best friend. "But he's also become a really good friend of mine. Well, at least I think he's my good friend. We hang out a lot at school and walk home together a few days a week. Plus, we text pretty often. But we never really hang out outside of school."

"What if we planned a group hangout one weekend?" Lily suggests. "Me, you, the rest of the P4F girls, and maybe Ali and your newspaper friends?"

"I like that idea a lot," Gracie says with a smile, glad she opened up to her friend. "Maybe I'll suggest it to him on Monday."

"Fun!" Lily says, grabbing a couple of bags of chips. "He seemed super nice at the fashion show. I can't wait to get to know him more."

"Same," Gracie confirms, adding a container of pretzels to the shopping cart. "The group hangout would be so much fun. We just have to make sure things are good with the P4F girls first."

"Of course," Lily says with a nod. "That's the most important thing."

"So, we have the snacks covered," Gracie says, looking down at the stuffed shopping cart. "What do you think for Shabbat dinner?"

"This idea may be sort of out there," Lily says, "but my mom had this special brisket she would make whenever any of us were feeling kind of bummed out. She called it her magic brisket because she swore it cured any problem. I had to do some digging to find it, but my dad found the recipe scribbled down in an old notebook of hers that we kept."

Lily pulls out her phone to show Gracie the picture of the recipe penned in dark blue ink on a piece of wide-ruled notebook paper.

"There's no pressure to make it or anything," Lily quickly says. "It would take us, like, three hours. I just thought . . . maybe it's just what we need right now."

"No," Gracie says, touched that her friend went to the lengths to find the recipe and that she wants to share it with Gracie and the rest of the P4F girls. "We *have* to make it. Let's get all the ingredients! It's only twelve thirty. We have plenty of time, plus Mimi is always up for a cooking adventure."

"Great!" Lily says, before quietly adding, "This is going to be my first time having her brisket recipe since she . . . you know. I'm glad I'm sharing it with you guys."

"I bet it's going to be the best brisket ever," Gracie says, wrapping an arm around Lily. "I can't wait to see its magical powers!"

"Is it ready?!" Gracie eagerly asks, peering over her mimi's shoulder as she pulls the brisket out of the oven and places it onto the kitchen counter. "It smells *so* good."

"It looks pretty ready to me," her mimi says, before grabbing a fork out of the drawer. "And it *smells* divine. Lily, why don't you try a bite and tell us what you think?"

"My mom always said it was ready when it was fork tender," Lily says, grabbing a fork of her own and gently tapping the hunk of meat. "Hmm, I think this could actually go in for about twenty more minutes? If that's okay with you . . ."

"It's your mom's recipe!" Gracie reminds her with a laugh. "Who cares if it's okay with Mimi and me?"

Her mimi checks the time on the microwave. "The girls will be here in fifteen minutes," she says, carefully placing the brisket back in the oven. "Twenty more minutes should be perfect timing."

Gracie bites down on her lower lip, her heart rate increasing speed as she awaits the arrival of her friends. "I *really* hope this brisket works its magic," she says. "I just want everything to go back to normal so badly."

"Same," Lily says. "But I promise. This brisket recipe has *never* failed me."

Before they know it, the doorbell rings and Maya is standing at Gracie's front door with a chocolate cake in hand.

"Hi, y'all," she says, handing Gracie the cake. "I baked this for tonight. It's a Texas sheet cake. I don't know if you've had it before, but it's my favorite. My friends and I used to have it any time there was a special occasion back at home."

"Thanks, Maya!" Gracie exclaims, grateful for her friend's gesture. "This looks *so* good. Also, your outfit is great. Are the overalls new?"

"Yeah," Maya says, smiling down at the brown overalls she has on over a turtleneck ivory sweater. "I found it thrifting last week."

"It's so you," Lily says with a smile. "And you tied the whole outfit together so well with the boot and the hat."

"You think?" Maya asks, toying with the rim of her ivory rancher hat. "I wasn't sure if it was too matchy, and normally I would ask the group what y'all think, but . . . you know."

"Yeah," Lily says with an understanding smile. "We know."

Maya follows the girls into the kitchen as Gracie sets the cake onto the counter.

"So, uh, has anyone heard from Ava and Sophia?" Gracie asks. "I know they're only one minute late as of now, but they're still coming, right?"

"Yeah, I talked to them this morning," Maya says. "They're definitely still coming."

"Cool," Lily says with a smile. "I'm sure they'll be here soon."

"Yep," Gracie says, her eyes glued to the clock. "Can't wait."

There's a brief, awkward silence, then Maya wraps her arms around her two friends.

"I'm sorry, but I just missed y'all so much," she says. "Can we just go back to normal please? Things got so out of hand with that silly fight. I know nobody really meant what they said."

"I am *so* up for things going back to normal," Gracie says, feeling like a million pounds was just swiftly lifted off her chest. "Let's just hope Sophia and Ava feel the same."

"I'm sure they will," Lily says, before nervously adding, "I mean, they agreed to come tonight. That's a good sign. Right?"

"Definitely," Maya says with an enthusiastic nod. "By the way, what's that smell? Something smells so good!"

"It's Lily's mom's magic brisket recipe," Gracie's mimi cuts in as she makes her way into the kitchen. "And it should be ready right about . . . *now*."

She pulls the baking dish out of the oven and sets it on the kitchen table as the delicious meaty smell of the brisket fills the house.

"Brisket?!" Maya excitedly asks, her ivory cowboy boots making a clanking sound as she bounces up and down on the hardwood floors of Gracie's kitchen. "We used to have brisket all the time at barbecues in Texas. My mouth is already watering."

"Lily, I seriously hope this is ready, because I'm going to need a bite right now," Gracie says. "This smells incredible."

"Let's see," Lily says, grabbing the same fork she used to test it the first time. "It definitely *smells* ready. I just need it to pass the fork test."

Lily gently taps on the hunk of meat and smiles as a small piece seamlessly flakes off.

"Yep." She nods. "It's ready."

"That's great news," Gracie's mimi says with a smile. "I can't *wait* to try. But for now, I'm going to head upstairs to get tomorrow's paint party set up!" She plants a quick kiss atop Gracie's head and makes her way upstairs.

"Okay, so you think I can try it?" Gracie asks Lily after her mimi has made her way out of the kitchen. "It's ready?"

"Definitely," Lily confirms with a smile. "Have a bite!"

Gracie grabs a fork of her own and tries a piece, the rich, tender meat and Lily's mom's signature mix of seasoning spices causing a full flavor explosion in her mouth.

"Whoa!" Gracie exclaims. "I see why you guys thought this was magic. It might be the best thing I've ever tasted in my whole life."

"What's the best thing you've ever tasted?" Ava asks as she strolls into the kitchen with Sophia towing closely behind her. "It smells *divine* in here."

Ava and Sophia both look great. Ava is dressed in a black mini sweater dress over a puff-sleeved white button-down, and Sophia is in one of her new signature dance looks with baggy white sweatpants, a white hoodie, and black-and-white Air Force 1s. All Gracie wants to do is chat about their looks. She wishes this annoying weirdness wasn't in the way.

"Oh, hi," Gracie says, gulping hard. "How'd you get in?"

"The front door was open," Sophia says with a shrug, her hands tucked into the pockets of her baggy white sweatpants. "We let ourselves in."

"Hi, y'all!" Maya exclaims, pulling them both in for a big hug. "Guess what! Lily and Gracie made Lily's mom's magic brisket."

"Ah," Ava says, her head slowly bobbing in a knowing nod. "So that explains the divine scent."

"So, uh, what's magic about it?" Sophia asks, cautiously eyeing the delicious-looking dish. "Besides the yummy smell."

"Well, when my mom was alive, she would make this whenever something was wrong," Lily explains, her voice soft. "Whether you had the flu or you were having a bad day, this brisket was always the fix."

"Hi, girls," Gracie's mama says, making her way into the kitchen. "You ready for Shabbat dinner? The sun is about to set."

"Ms. Anna is right—er, unerring," Ava confirms, taking a look at her dainty gold watch. "The sun is scheduled to set in ten minutes. It is *imperative* that we light the candles now if we want to make Shabbat."

"Wonderful," Gracie's mama says with a smile, grabbing the brisket dish with oven mitts and taking it to the dining room where the table is already set with the rest of the sides Lily and Gracie helped her mimi whip up this afternoon. "Wow, this looks like a delicious spread."

"It really does," Maya says with wide eyes. "Did you make everything yourselves?"

"The challah is actually from a bakery a few blocks away," Gracie says. "They make a really good challah. But everything else we made."

"You girls ready to kick off your Shabbat tradition?" her mama asks, a lighter in hand.

Gracie looks around at her friends and they all quietly nod that they're ready.

"Okay," her mama says, lighting the two candles on the table. "I'm going to head upstairs to help Ms. Brie finish setting up the paint party. Just give us a shout if you need anything."

Things definitely still feel weird about them, but the Shabbat ritual seamlessly flows between the girls. Once Gracie's mama heads upstairs, they all immediately place their hands over their eyes. After completing her third eye-covering motion, Gracie knows it's her turn to recite "A Friend," by Gillian Jones. Gracie begins reciting the profound words that she's shared so many times over the past few months and everything is going seemingly well, until suddenly she forgets the third line in the poem.

"They will not . . . um," she stammers, her face turning red as her mind goes blank. "Not . . . uh . . ."

"They will not flee when bad times are here." Beside her, Lily gives her hand a squeeze and continues performing the poem where Gracie left off, immediately jogging Gracie's memory. Gracie joins in, relieved, now reciting the poem in unison with her friend. Then, to her surprise, Maya grabs her other hand and joins in. By the end of the poem, all five girls are holding hands and reciting the last line together.

"I'll go ahead and say it," Ava says, serving herself a large heaping of the brisket. "Gracie forgetting that third line might be the most *marvelous* mistake anyone has ever made. How did we not think to recite that together sooner?"

"I agree," Lily says with grin to Gracie. "It was so much more special that way."

"I'm glad it worked out for the best," Gracie says. "I don't know what happened! I obviously know all the words. I think I got in my own head thinking about friendship and you all, and just wanting . . ."

". . . wanting things to not be weird anymore?" Sophia finishes Gracie's sentence, a small smile on her face. "Because I feel the same."

"Really?" Gracie is so overjoyed, she thinks she might cry. "Sophia, I really didn't mean what I said. I don't even know why I said it! I know you care about us just as much as you care about your New York life."

"I know you do," Sophia says. "And I'm sorry I was so rude about your Poconos trip. I know it's not realistic for all of us to do absolutely everything together all the time."

"I really wish we could," Gracie says, looking around the table. "And I'm sorry for maybe taking the business thing a little too far. I know it's supposed to be fun above all else."

"In your defense, it would have been fun if we had more time to devote to it," Ava says. "We're just so busy right now. I think your charity idea seems more . . . *feasible*."

"Same," Sophia agrees. "Is everyone ready to be done with the weirdness?"

"Yep," the girls say at the same time, giggling as they toast with their apple cider.

"Now, I have an idea," Gracie suggests. "How about we finish dinner, have the great-looking sheet cake Maya got for us, then just enjoy our night with no business—or charity—talk?"

"That sounds like a *fabulous* idea," Ava says, heading into the kitchen. "I'll go grab the cake!"

The girls spend the rest of the night stuffing their faces with delicious food and catching up on everything they missed over the past week of weirdness. Between the belly laughs at inside jokes and heart-to-hearts, things finally start feeling normal between the girls.

When time finally comes for them to go to sleep in the sleeping bags Gracie's mama set up for them in Gracie's bedroom, Ava notices the copy of the *Ardmore Aardvark Gazette* lying on Gracie's desk.

"Wait," Ava says, grabbing the newspaper. "Gracie, I can't believe we didn't discuss the fashion feature!"

The girls excitedly huddle around Ava as she carefully scans each of Gracie's looks juxtaposed next to Grandma Zoey's.

"Gracie, you crushed it," Sophia says, her eyes wide with awe. "Also, your Grandma Zoey had the best style! I bet she and my baba would have been friends."

"Yeah, I wish I got to spend more time with her," Gracie says. "But this made me feel so close to her."

"It seems like you two had a *lot* in common," Maya points out. "Your styles may have been different, but the same passion was definitely there for both of you."

"She's right," Lily says with a nod. "It's obvious the two of you just have a natural knack for thinking outside the box with your style."

"Thanks, girls," Gracie says, coming in for a group hug. "Not to be all corny here, but I really am so happy to have us hanging like normal again."

The girls join in the hug and agree that they will never let weirdness last between them for this long again. By the time Gracie slips into her sleeping bag at the end of the night, she feels calmer than she has in weeks. *Maybe Lily's mom's brisket really* is *magic,* she thinks as she dozes off.

fourteen

"Who wants pancakes?" Gracie's mimi says cheerily as the girls file into the kitchen in the morning. "Now, I don't want to toot my own horn here, but I have prepared *quite* the breakfast feast for you girls."

"I'll toot it for her," Max says from the kitchen table. "These pancakes rule."

"Max, when did you get back?" Gracie asks, serving herself a combination of banana and chocolate chip pancakes, mixed berry pancakes, and her mimi's signature Funfetti pancakes. "Didn't you have a sleepover at Tao's house last night?"

"He did," her mama says from where she's seated next to him. "But we picked him up at nine this morning. You girls slept in late! It's already eleven."

"It was nice," Ava says, the feather trim on her silk pajamas dancing around as she stretches her arms up high above her head and lets out a yawn. "I can usually keep up with my busy schedule, but it has had me exhausted the past few weeks."

"You weren't kidding," Sophia says to Gracie's mimi as she scans the expansive breakfast buffet she has laid out on the counter. "This really is a feast!"

"Wait," Maya says, a smile making its way across her face as she carefully scans the chocolate French toast. "Did you . . ."

"Talk to your dad?" Gracie's mimi completes her thought. "Yes! One night when all of us parents got together a while back, I remember him mentioning how he has this great recipe for turning Texas sheet cake into French toast. He told me he used to make it for you and your friend after slumber parties, so I shot him a text last night as soon as you brought over the cake."

"Oh my gosh!" Maya says, careful not to get any syrup on her white Victorian-style nightgown as she drizzles syrup over her plate. "I haven't had sheet cake French toast since we moved here."

"I've had two slices already," Max chimes in. "It is *very* good."

"I'm sure it is," Lily says, taking a seat at the table and carefully rolling up the sleeves on her long-sleeved lilac-colored silk pajama top before cutting her first bite. "Whoa, Maya, this is delicious."

"Yep," Sophia agrees after taking a bite of her own French toast from the seat next to Lily's. "Who would have thought sheet cake would make good French toast?"

"Shoot, I didn't get any!" Gracie exclaims, flicking a colorful pancake crumb off her pink-and-black checkered onesie. "When I finish this plate, I'll go grab one."

"I can get you some from here," Ava offers from where she's standing by the counter. "There's only one left. It's all yours."

"Thanks, Aves," Gracie says with an appreciative smile.

Once the girls finish the delicious breakfast feast, they head upstairs to do some painting. Gracie originally wanted to get straight to brainstorming ideas, but her mimi suggested they do the paint party first.

"Nothing gets the creative juices flowing like some painting," Gracie's mimi says to the girls. "Just head up to the studio and paint your hearts out. *Then* you can sit around and talk charity ideas once your minds are feeling nice and loose."

As always, Gracie's mimi is right. The girls wind up spending hours up in the studio, getting lost in their respective masterpieces—Gracie, a portrait of a neon pink guitar; Lily, a series of white hearts neatly painted over a lilac backdrop; Sophia, a more abstract take on the New York City skyline; Maya, a portrait of her farm back in Texas; and Ava, a replica of a Monet piece she saw while on vacation with her family in Europe.

By the time they finally make their way down to the Gracie's living room that afternoon, they're buzzing with the creative energy necessary for an epic brainstorm session.

"So," Sophia begins as she sinks into the super comfy bright orange couch. "Is it time we talk about . . . you know?"

"The charity?" Ava smiles. "I think it is, indeed, time."

"You sure?" Gracie nervously asks. "I *really* don't want to be pushing anyone into anything. Seriously."

"No," Sophia reassures. "You're not. The charity idea sounds cool. Tell us more about what you were thinking."

"Well, I was hoping we could flesh it out together," Gracie begins. "Maybe we could start by picking a cause, then think of something we could do to help that's also related to fashion."

"Got it," Ava says with a nod, jumping up from her seat on the couch. "Give me *one* minute."

In the time the girls exchange confused looks, Ava is already back with her notebook and a pen in hand. "We should keep a log of all the ideas we think of," she says as she opens the book. "I would write it in my phone, but multiple studies show that handwriting your notes is better for cognition."

"Are we just going to do one cause?" Lily asks. "Like, are we going to pick one and stick to it, or will we do different charity projects for different causes?"

"I think we can see as we go," Gracie says. "But let's just pick one cause for now to start things off."

"Okay, so what are people thinking?" Ava asks, looking up from the notebook. "Anything off the top of anyone's head?"

"We could try more for disaster relief," Sophia suggests as Ava jots it down. "You know, like what we did for Maya's hometown. But we could find other towns that have natural disasters happening."

"Yeah, another idea is food pantries," Lily suggests. "I used to volunteer at one with my friends back in New York. They could use so much help."

"What if we did something for animals?" Maya asks as Ava quickly transcribes every word. "There are so many great animal-related charities."

"These are all *superb* options," Ava says, looking down at the list. "I don't think we could possibly go wrong. The question is, which one do we have the best fashion-related fundraising idea for?"

"I don't want to be pushy," Gracie says, carefully measuring her words. "So, if you don't like this idea, no big deal! For real. But I do have an idea that could go pretty well with animal rescue."

"What are you thinking, Gracie?" Lily asks with a gentle smile. "Tell us."

"What if we made cute animal accessories?" Gracie asks. "You know, like, fun collars and things like that. Then we could sell them and use the proceeds to benefit a local animal shelter."

"Plus, we could donate any of the items we don't sell to the shelter!" Maya exclaims. "No waste."

"It's a great idea," Sophia says. "Making animal accessories sounds so fun, and actually I think I have the perfect place in mind. There's a dog shelter my mom and I volunteer at sometimes right in our neighborhood. It's called Puppy Paradise. They take in neglected dogs all over Philadelphia and give them the love and attention they need."

Ava nods in agreement, placing her pen down. "I think we've got the idea."

"Yay!" Lily softly exclaims, a small smile making its way across her face. "This idea sounds amazing. Fashion is always fun, but it feels so much better when we're giving back."

"I agree," Maya says with a nod. "And I can't wait to make our own fun little pet accessories! I have a great dog collar design already coming together in my head."

"And I think this can be way less intense than the business," Gracie says. "We can just make the accessories when we feel like it and sell them at our own pace. And it doesn't even need to be an ongoing thing! We could just make one small capsule collection to start, and make more when and if we feel like it."

"This feels . . . more doable." Ava confesses. "I was really feeling stressed out about starting a business with everything else I have going on."

"I agree," Sophia says. "I mean, *nobody* is as stressed as you are, Ava. But even just trying to balance the business with P4F, homework, trips to New York, and hip-hop class was starting to feel like a lot."

"Yeah, it was okay at first," Lily quietly says. "But with

soccer season starting up and my cantor's class, I think things were slowly starting to get a bit unmanageable for me."

"I know what you mean, Lily," Maya says. "Things started feeling so stressful when my extracurriculars picked up too."

Gracie's chest tightens as she hears her friends discuss how they were feeling. She knows that she isn't solely to blame here, but she can't help but feel like a lot of their stress is her fault.

"I am so sorry if I made you all feel stressed," Gracie tells her friends, holding back a small wave of tears she feels coming on. "I was just excited and I guess it came out wrong."

Sophia and Maya reach their arms around Gracie from either side of her and give her a hug.

"Do *not* feel bad," Ava reassures. "We know you were just excited about it. It's not your fault we all congested our schedules."

"Seriously," Lily says. "You set aside all this time to devote to the business and we didn't do the same thing. We're to blame too. We shouldn't have committed when we didn't have the time."

"And don't forget *you* are the one who came up with this awesome charity idea!" Maya says. "This is the perfect solution. It's less stressful, it's fun, and we get to help so many cute animals."

The other girls enthusiastically nod in agreement, and Gracie relaxes a bit. She can already feel a difference in the air as they discuss this new idea. *This feels right*, she thinks.

"I'm glad you're all excited about this," Gracie says. "And actually, with the extra time I'll have in my schedule, I was thinking that maybe I should pick up an extracurricular at school too."

"Extremely *prudent* idea," Ava says. "My high school admissions counselor says high schools and subsequently colleges are all about extracurriculars. You already have P4F, but no harm in picking up another."

"I don't know much about college and high school applications," Maya says. "But I do know that extracurriculars are just fun! I'm excited for you, Gracie. You're going to have a great time."

"I agree," Sophia says. "I didn't do one until this year either. But starting hip-hop has changed my whole experience at school. I've made so many friends and met so many cool people I didn't even know went to Charis with Ava and me."

"I don't know *how* I would make friends if it wasn't for soccer and P4F," Lily chimes in. "I'm way too shy to just make friends at lunch or in class. Hanging with people outside of school just makes things easier."

"Do you have an extracurricular in mind, Gracie?" Sophia asks. "We can help you brainstorm options if you're on the fence."

"Actually," Gracie begins, "I think I have my mind pretty set on one . . . I've made some friends on the *Ardmore Aardvark Gazette* and Sue Ellen, the girl who interviewed me for my Best Dressed feature, offered me to be a fashion writer on there. It seems exactly like something I would have a blast doing."

"Excuse me," her mimi says, popping her head in from the kitchen. "Did I just hear my little girl say she's thinking of joining the school paper? I love this idea!"

Gracie's mama trails in behind her. "Oh, honey," she says. "You have always been a fantastic writer. And what better topic for you to write about than fashion?"

"Plus," Ava adds, "the newspaper will be great for promoting our charity! This could not have worked out more perfectly."

Gracie smiles and excitedly opens up her WhatsApp text thread with Ali.

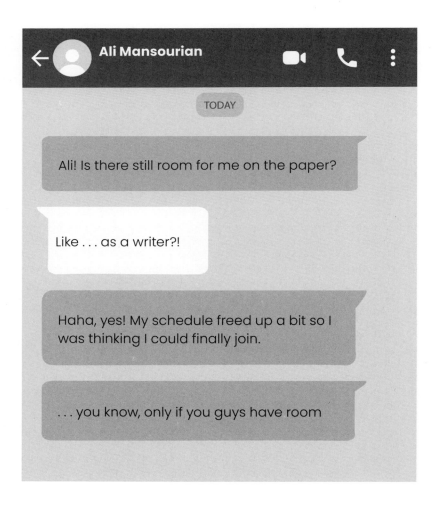

Ali Mansourian

TODAY

Ali! Is there still room for me on the paper?

Like . . . as a writer?!

Haha, yes! My schedule freed up a bit so I was thinking I could finally join.

. . . you know, only if you guys have room

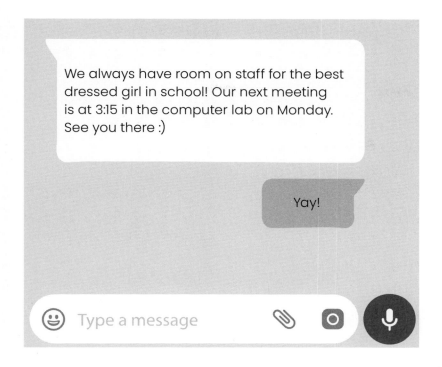

We always have room on staff for the best dressed girl in school! Our next meeting is at 3:15 in the computer lab on Monday. See you there :)

Yay!

Type a message

Gracie blushes and stuffs her phone back into the pocket of her pajamas before turning her attention back over to the girls, "Okay, so should we start working on some animal accessories?"

Her mama luckily has all of the supplies they need to create fun dog collars, from customizable charms to buckles to a wide array of weather-proof fabrics they can cut into thin slivers. The girls spend the rest of the day sewing and brainstorming names for their new charity initiative until they settle on a winner: Puppy Love.

fifteen

B y the time the girls get to Passion for Fashion class on Thursday, Gracie's mama has the dozens of dog collars they created for Puppy Love in a basket at the center of their white work table.

"So," she tells the girls, who are all seated around the table. "Since we have plenty of collars here, I was thinking we could spend today making a few specialty items you girls could include in your Puppy Love collection. I didn't have much yarn in the house, but we have plenty here in the store, along with some tough fabrics. How about some little sweaters and booties for dogs to wear as it starts to get colder?"

"Dog booties?!" Sophia exclaims. "That is the cutest thing I have ever heard."

"Sophia, if you want to make booties, I also have some rubber gripping here that I can show you how to put onto the bottom once the bootie is finished," Gracie's mama says. "I also did some research and printed out some patterns you girls can follow."

"I want to make booties too!" Maya says. "Ms. Anna, do you think it would be possible for me to embroider a little paisley print onto mine? I want to make them *cowboy* booties."

"Wait, Maya, that is the best idea ever!" Gracie says. "Maybe I could do doggie combat booties."

"I can turn my booties into Air Force 1s!" Sophia says, reaching for white fabric. "This is going to be awesome."

"I'm going to go in a different direction," Ava says. "Ms. Anna, do you think it would take way too long—erm, be way too time *intensive*—if I wanted to make a dog sweater? It could be a small one, like for the size of a small puppy. I like that blush-colored yarn there, so I was thinking I could use it and decorate it with those red pom poms."

"Not too long at all, honey," Gracie's mama reassures Ava. "Remember? No more time crunch! The charity is more relaxed. Take all the time you need to make what you really want to make."

"Ah," Ava says, visibly relaxing. "Okay, great. I'm going to make a dog sweater. Do you have any patterns for that?"

"I *do*," Gracie's mama says, heading over toward her office. "I'll be back in a minute."

"Okay, my idea is kind of silly," Lily says. "But ever since we came up with Puppy Love, I've been following a bunch of puppy style accounts on Instagram and seeing all of these puppies with little winter scarves. I was thinking I would make a few of those! They probably will fall right off the dogs, but they look really cute on them in holiday cards and stuff."

"I think that's a *dazzling* idea," Ava says. "My friend Isabella had this little red scarf on her dog when I stopped by their house for Christmas last year, and it was seriously the most adorable thing ever."

"Great," Lily says with a smile, reaching for a pale blue skein of yarn. "I think I'm going to make a bunch of them in different colors. They should be pretty easy to make."

"Yes, Lily, scarves are simple enough," Gracie's mama confirms when she returns with the pattern for Ava. "You could even finger knit them if you'd like! I know you like finger knitting."

"That's true," Lily says with a smile. "Oh, this is going to be so fun."

"So, Sophia," Gracie begins as pulls some black fabric to her sewing machine to create her first combat bootie. "When's your next hip-hop recital?"

"And can we please come?" Maya asks, clapping her hands excitedly. "I want to see your performance so badly."

"The hip-hop girls performed at an assembly at school last week," Ava says, carefully paying attention to the knit as she cross-references the pattern Gracie's mama showed her. "And, trust me, it is *worth* checking out. They were *otherworldly*. And Sophia was the star! They had her front and center!"

"They only did that because Leila Mosef was out," Sophia says, her face turning bright red. "I'm not the *star*."

"Well, star or not—you are a *masterful* dancer," Ava insists. "I saw it with my own eyes!"

"Thanks, Aves," Sophia says, still blushing. "If you all really want to come to a performance, our next recital is next Friday. My dad and my baba are even driving here from New York to be there!"

"Mama, can I please go?" Gracie asks. "Please!"

Her mama laughs before answering, "Of course! Sophia, if it's okay with you, I would love to come too. After Ava's review, I need to see this performance live."

"Of course you can come, Ms. Anna," Sophia says. "I'm sure my mom will be happy to see you."

"I'm texting my parents right now to see if I can come," Maya says, typing quickly on her phone. ". . . and my mom just said yes!"

"I just got a yes from my dad too," Lily says, looking down at her phone. "Sophia, I bet you're going to be amazing."

"She really is amazing," Ava says. "Just wait until you see her."

"I hope so," Sophia says, nervously biting her lower lip. "Now, can we please change the subject before I get any more embarrassed?"

"Sure," Maya says with a laugh, giving Sophia comforting pat on the back. "Gracie, how was your first week on the newspaper?"

Gracie has been waiting for the right moment to show them the rough draft she wrote up for the *Ardmore Aardvark Gazette*.

"Funny you should ask," she begins. "If you guys are interested, I just finished up the first article I'm going to submit to Sue Ellen tomorrow. It's about P4F. It's still super rough, but do you want me to read it out loud?"

"Wait, you didn't tell me that you finished your rough draft!" Lily says, her eyes widening as a sheepish smile makes its way across her face. "Yeah, read it out loud!"

The rest of the girls agree and Gracie pulls the email up from her phone and begins to read.

WHEN FASHION TURNS TO FAMILY
By Grace Alexander-Cline

My name is Grace Alexander-Cline, and I have always felt like an outsider with pretty much everyone other than my brother and my moms. I remember sitting at the kitchen table with my family at the beginning of this past summer, feeling like I was going to vomit because I was so terrified of going back to school. But then my mama suggested I join a class she was offering at her store, Zoey's Closet. The class was called Passion for Fashion, or P4F, and my mama thought I could maybe make some friends who shared my love for fashion. I agreed, but I was doubtful. Making friends has never really been my thing. How was this class going to be any different?

Then I got there and I met these four girls. The five of us could not be more different in terms of our style, our backgrounds, and even our personalities. But we share a connection that goes deeper than all of that.

When people think of fashion, they think of the clothes we wear on our bodies. But to me, it has become so much more than that. My love for fashion has connected me to my very best friends—a group of girls I would have probably never crossed paths with otherwise. We may be different in so many ways, but we are the same in all the ways that matter. For example, we all love finding ways to use our passion for fashion to give back. When my friend Maya's hometown got hit with a hurricane, we came together to host a charity fashion show to raise money for the town's recovery. Now, we have come together to start a new charity initiative called Puppy Love, and our plan is to sell a line of dog accessories we're creating and donate the money to the animal shelter Puppy Paradise.

But honestly? My favorite thing about my P4F friends isn't how we are the same. It's how we treat our differences. We appreciate each other's unique sense of style and have fun learning about each other's background. As the months go by and we get closer, they feel less like friends and more like family.

Upon finishing her reading, Gracie nervously looks up from her phone to find all her friends staring back at her with glassy eyes. *Oh no*, she thinks. *Do they hate it?* But suddenly, all four of them drop their projects on the table and pounce on her for a big group hug.

"Are you kidding me?" Sophia asks, wiping a tear off her face. "Gracie, that was beautiful!"

"Seriously." Lily nods through sniffles. "It was so nice."

"And you remembered to plug the charity!" Ava exclaims. "Oh, Gracie, it was perfect. I don't even have a better vocab word. It really was just perfect."

"It really was!" Maya exclaims, wiping off a stream of tears. "I love y'all."

"I love you all too," Gracie says, still being held tightly at the center of her friends' group hug.

She looks around and can't believe the one decision to join a class at Zoey's Closet landed her here with the best friends in the world.

about the author

Tina Wells is the author of twelve books, including the bestselling tween fiction series *Mackenzie Blue*, and its spinoff series, *The Zee Files*. She is also a business strategist, advisor, and the founder of RLVNT Media, a multimedia content venture serving entrepreneurs, tweens, and culturists with authentic representation. She has been featured on TV and in multiple publications, including *O, The Oprah Magazine, Marie Claire, Forbes, USA Today*, NPR, and the *New York Times. Gracie Opens Shop* is the third book in the *Stitch Clique* series. Tina lives on the East Coast but likes to travel and share her passion to encourage and uplift young people.